ELISABETH BERESFORD

The Mysterious Island

Illustrated by Joanna Carey

'And then a very strange thing happened. With a flurry the mist curled away as though an unseen hand had drawn aside a filmy curtain and there . . . jutting out from the rocky foreshore, was a castle which seemed to be floating on the sea.'

This brief vision of the castle remains with Billy through all his troubles – quarantine for Ben, his dog, and finding a home and work for himself and Grandpa – and strangely enough, it is the mysterious castle that finally provides Billy with the answers to his problems . . .

D0774248

ELISABETH BERESFORD

The Mysterious Island

A Magnet Book

Also by Elisabeth Beresford
in Magnet Books:

The Animals Nobody Wanted
Knights of the Cardboard Castle
Stephen and the Shaggy Dog
Toby's Luck
The Island Bus
The Secret Railway
The Happy Ghost
The Treasure Hunters
The Tovers

First published in Great Britain 1984
by Methuen Children's Books Ltd
Magnet paperback edition first published 1986
by Methuen Children's Books Ltd
11 New Fetter Lane, London EC4P 4EE
Text copyright © 1982 by Elisabeth Beresford
Illustrations copyright © 1984 by Methuen Children's Books Ltd
Reproduced, printed and bound in Great Britain by
Hazell Watson & Viney Limited,
Member of the BPCC Group,
Aylesbury, Bucks

ISBN 0 416 52110 X

Contents

To Ben (Vincent)
and Boddie (Parker)

1 · Billy Goes To Sea

'Something'll come along, you'll see, said Mr. Luft putting down a glass and a cup on the café table. Billy nodded and sucked the straw in his can which was half full of warm, flat coke. He waited until his grandfather wasn't looking and then took a saucer off the table next door, put it down on the ground and then poured the coke into it. Ben, who had been lying like a rolled-up grey and white carpet under Billy's chair, edged forward, put out a long pink tongue and began to drink. He was a noisy eater (and drinker) and went 'slurp SLURP slurp', but Grandpa was reading the paper and didn't notice.

'Although there's not a lot of jobs going round here, I must admit,' Grandpa went on. He blew on his cup of tea and then sipped, making a noise not unlike Ben. Counting under his breath, Billy waited for what he knew would come next. He'd got to 'eight' when Grandpa slapped the paper down on the table and slid his spectacles off the top of his head and onto his nose. 'Perhaps we'd better move on a bit,' he said. 'What do *you* think, Billy?'

Grandpa had politely been asking Billy what he

thought about things since Billy was five years old which was years and years ago.

'Well . . . ' Billy said slowly and sighed.

Sometimes he wished that he and Grandpa could settle down somewhere for a while. It was quite fun travelling round and seeing different places and meeting new people, but it also meant never getting used to anywhere or making proper friends.

'Perhaps a bit further down the coast,' said Grandpa, 'we could try one of those big seaside towns. Sure to be a lot of work going there at the start of the holiday season. I'll soon find something. Always did fancy this part of the world.'

But then Grandpa said that about anywhere they went. It wasn't really his fault that they were always moving on, it was just that the jobs he got never seemed to last for long. Billy stared across the sea front trying to remember all the different kinds of work Grandpa had done. The most unusual job had been when he'd been general handyman in a circus. Billy had enjoyed that because he'd been able to help too by looking after some of the animals. Not the *big* ones, of course – like the elephants and the lions – but the little monkeys and the performing dogs.

Billy's hand went down to Ben's rough coat. He had tried to teach Ben some of the circus tricks, although Ben hadn't taken the slightest notice. But then he never did, he just went deaf, shut his eyes – as

far as one could see his eyes under his thick fringe – planted his enormous paws far apart and apparently believed he had become invisible. When Billy was small he used to ride on Ben's back, but he was too big to do that now. Ben licked Billy's wrist and panted heavily, his sides heaving.

'Going to be a real scorcher of a day,' Grandpa said, 'not the sort of day to look for work, really. We could buy some sandwiches and have a picnic on the beach. What do you think, Billy?'

'All right,' said Billy. He never said a lot because Grandpa talked enough for both of them. Grandpa finished his tea, Ben slurped up the last drop of his cola and Billy counted up their luggage. There wasn't a great deal of it, just two medium sized travelling bags for himself and Grandpa and a smaller one for Ben which held his spare collar, his feeding bowl and his special shawl. This was a very old, threadbare piece of material to which Ben was deeply devoted, and if it ever got left behind on their travels, he would put back his head and howl and howl until he got it back.

Grandpa paid for the drinks and picked up two of the bags while Billy took the third and Ben's lead. Ben didn't really need it as he always walked close to heel, sometimes so close that his large paws came down quite heavily on Billy's feet. But in a lot of places through which they had travelled there were

signs saying 'Keep Dogs On Lead', so they did it just to be on the safe side. Ben didn't seem to mind one way or the other, although when the lead was clipped onto his collar he would turn his head up and look through his fringe in a way which said quite clearly, 'you're *daft*.'

But at that moment he was too hot to bother. He just panted heavily against Billy's legs, giving a tremendous sigh every time they had to stop at the edge of the curb because of the slow-moving traffic. There were crowds of people about already although it was still very early in the morning and the air smelt of petrol, popcorn and chips.

'Look at that,' Grandpa said in Billy's ear. 'That's a fine looking craft. It reminds me of the time I sailed up the Windward Islands. Now that's what I call a *proper* boat.'

Billy and Ben stared in the direction in which he was pointing, but all they could see was a long, low, rather shabby ship with one yellow funnel and some flaking white paintwork. She was tied up close to the harbour wall, rolling slightly with the tide. A red crane was winching some large packing cases on board and suddenly made such a dreadful screeching noise that a line of seagulls on top of a warehouse roof flew up into the hazy sky going 'Ow-ow-ow-ooooow' with their necks stuck out and their webbed feet hanging down. Ben went 'Hm hm hm' at the back of his throat and lay down on the hot pavement. Billy rather wished he could do the same thing as they had already been walking for quite a long time and the soles of his flip-flops were getting very warm.

'She's seen a bit of travel,' Grandpa went on. He never minded if people didn't reply to what he was saying. He felt for his old pipe and fitted it upside down into the corner of his mouth. 'Travelled a few thousand miles I daresay. Why I recall the time when . . .'

It never was to be recalled, however, as at that moment a large lorry pulled away from the quay, scattering the gulls once again, and a notice board came into view. 'Waterfall Seaways Ltd. Mystery Day Trips. Adults £15–00 return. Children half price. Sailing 7.55 a.m. SHARP.' A few people were already standing hopefully at the end of the gang plank and it was at that *exact* moment that Grandpa got one of his Great Ideas.

'How about a day off? I've always wanted to go on one of those mystery trips!'

'Now?' asked Billy cautiously.

He wasn't too sure he liked the look of the ship as much as Grandpa did, added to which he'd never been to sea. Although if one were going on a trip, today was perfect for it as there was hardly a ripple on the pale blue water.

'Now as ever is. No time like the present,' said

Grandpa slinging the holdalls onto his shoulder as if he was a sailor with a kitbag. 'I always *knew* something would come along. Off we go.'

'But . . .' said Billy.

It was no use; Grandpa had got an idea into his head again and he was off. Billy and Ben looked at each other and then Ben heaved himself to his feet, gave himself a tremendous shake so that dust flew in all directions, and they set off towards the ship.

Seen close to she certainly looked larger, but also a great deal shabbier as her paintwork was both rusty and dirty and she smelt quite strongly of salt, oil and fish. Ben sniffed deeply and Billy watched the way the boat rocked from side to side even in the flat, oily water of the harbour. There was a girl selling tickets from a small kiosk. She didn't seem very interested in what she was doing and when Grandpa asked her what time they would be coming back she said:

'I dunno. Depends on the tides.'

'And where does she sail *to*?'

'It's a mystery tour, in'it?' said the girl sounding quite cross as she took Grandpa's money and handed over the tickets. She turned away and began using the telephone so there was nothing else to do but walk over to the gang plank. One or two people were starting to arrive and look about hopefully and Grandpa immediately decided to get on board ahead of them.

'Best to get good seats for'ard,' he said out of the corner of his mouth.

Billy, who was dreaming away on his feet, opened his mouth to ask what that meant, but Grandpa was already halfway up the gang plank so Billy and Ben followed after him. The smell was a great deal stronger on board and Ben gave one of his enormous sneezes so that his whiskers blew out sideways.

For'ard turned out to be the front end of the ship where there were some seats bolted to the deck.

'Make yourselves ship-shape,' said Grandpa, who was becoming more and more like a sailor himself every minute. 'I'll see if there's any grub to be had. Can't sail on an empty stomach.'

Billy wasn't too sure if he would sail too well on a full one, but Grandpa had already hurried off and when he returned with some cheese rolls and cups of coffee Billy found that he was quite hungry after all. They munched in silence – watching the quay side which was getting quite lively now with lorries, cars and people. Ben heaved himself into the shade, sighed a bit and then slept. It may have been his example or the early start to the day or just the heat, but Billy found himself nodding off until everything faded away into silence.

But not for long. Suddenly there were three ear-splitting blasts overhead from the siren, wisps of grey smoke were coming out of the funnel and the engines had begun to thud steadily, enormous ropes were being thrown back from the quay to the deck and a great gush of water boiled and bubbled out from underneath the boat. All the gulls took to the sky and some children on the harbour wall began to run along it waving and cheering as they tried to keep up. There is something very exciting about a ship leaving harbour and Billy and Grandpa made for the rail.

'It's going *backwards*' Billy said.

'*She*,' said Grandpa. 'Ships are always *Shes*. And she's going astern – it's the only way she *can* get out. If she went straight on she'd be halfway up the main street by now, you daft ha'porth!'

Billy grinned and knelt down beside Ben who was making 'hm hm' noises at the back of his throat.

'We're going to sea,' Billy explained, 'we're off for a *whole* day. . .'

But as things were to turn out they were going to be at sea for a great deal longer than *that* . . .

2 · Ben In Danger

There were quite a lot of people on board and as Grandpa had soon dozed off with his empty pipe sticking out of the corner of his mouth, Billy went off to talk to some of them.

'Isn't it exciting sailing on a mystery tour?' a plump woman said, patting her face with a handkerchief. Although they were now well and truly at sea as the coastline had long since vanished it was still very hot, even the slight breeze was warm as it made the flag snap from side to side.

'I'm wondering if even the Captain knows where we're headed,' replied her husband gloomily. 'If you ask me, we're in for some difficult weather. Care to have a look through my binoculars, young man?'

He handed them over and showed Billy how to adjust them, but it was just like looking into a milkshake, there was nothing to see but thick, swirling mist with here and there a flickering shadow of a seabird as it darted across Billy's line of vision.

'That's a real sea mist, that is,' the man said, 'and the sun's not strong enough yet to burn it off. What's more, if you ask me . . .' nobody had, but he was obviously the kind of person who liked to look on the black side of things, 'they're having some sort of trouble with the engines. I can hear that something's going wrong with them.'

The woman gave a small moan and sat down, mopping her face more than ever.

'If you ask me,' the man went on, 'we're in for trouble with a capital T. Mark my words.'

Before Billy could ask him whether he meant they were going to be shipwrecked or have to take to the lifeboats, the engine room bell started clanging and almost immediately afterwards the sound of the engines changed and seemed to become very much less noisy.

'Told you so,' the man said, looking quite pleased about it, 'we've lost power. Now we shall see what we shall see. Come along, Mavis, better have a cup of tea before they run out. It's going to turn into a mystery day *and* night trip if you ask me!'

Billy didn't feel in the least scared, only excited. It was still flat calm and it gave him an odd feeling to be surrounded by the hot, swirling white mist which coiled and billowed over the water. Overhead, the ship's foghorn was booming steadily, but it too sounded strange as it was muffled one moment and then louder the next. Most of the travellers were now leaning over the rails and talking to each other and shaking their heads, but Grandpa only opened one pale blue eye and cocked his head to one side as he listened to what Billy had to tell him.

'Probably had trouble with a cylinder, so she'll lose a bit of power and have to make for the nearest harbour. She's changing course now. Feel the tilt on the deck?'

'Where would the nearest port be?'

'Blessed if I can tell you, not knowing the tides and currents. It could be French France though!'

'Cor!' Billy's eyes shone. This was something like an adventure. At one of the many schools he had been to for a short time there had been a plan for his class to go to France on a day trip, but he and Grandpa had moved on before it had happened. He screwed up his eyes and tried to peer ahead, but it was some while before a vague shape began to appear and at the same time there was a loud clicking noise overhead and a voice boomed out.

'Ladies and Gentlemen, this is Captain Smith speaking. I regret to tell you that owing to a slight technical difficulty we shall have to put into the port of Le Huquet for a short time. Passengers will not be allowed ashore. We're sorry for this inconvenience. Thank you.'

Everybody started talking at once as they lined the rails to watch the shadowy shapes ahead turn into cliffs and then a round, floating buoy with a clanging bell on top of it came into muzzy view and shortly

after that a bright orange fishing boat went chugging past. A long harbour wall seemed to appear suddenly out of the sea and the mist cleared a little and Le Huquet came into sight. It didn't look very big, all the houses were huddled together and to one side there were some large warehouses. It wasn't unlike the small British port they had left, and yet there was something about it that made it very French.

'Cor,' said Billy again. 'I wish we *could* go ashore.'

'Not a chance,' said Grandpa, joining him at the rail. 'It'd be against regulations. Just listen to the racket.'

There was enough of it. Ships were hooting at each other, everybody seemed to be arguing and throwing their hands up in the air, the cars and vans were using their horns and even the French seagulls seemed to make more noise on this side of the Channel.

The gang plank was let down and a couple of the ship's crew hurried down onto the quay and at once some men in uniform came hurrying up to them and everybody started talking until they moved off in a group and vanished into one of the warehouses.

Most of the passengers didn't seem to mind that the Mystery Tour had been diverted to a small French port, but one or two grumbled quite a bit. Billy sighed and wished that now he was in spitting distance he could at least put one foot ashore so that he could tell any friend he might meet that he had been abroad. But there were two French policemen standing at the foot of the gang plank so there wasn't a chance. However, there was plenty to watch on shore and in the harbour and when the loudspeaker was switched on again and a voice told them that food and drinks would be free even the grumblers shut up.

'It's as good as a cruise, this is,' Grandpa said.

He had made himself very comfortable by turning one of the hold-alls into a pillow and taking off his shoes. Billy joined a group who were being taken on a conducted tour of the ship and Ben edged himself into the shade under Grandpa's seat and snored softly. So the time passed very pleasantly until there was a sudden bustle of activity from the engine room and a steady throb-throb started up.

'Off we go,' said Grandpa as Billy, with some black grease marks on his face and T-shirt came clattering along the deck.

'It *was* a cylinder,' Billy said rather thickly through the hamburger he was chewing. Being at sea makes you very hungry. 'One of the engine crew told me all about it. He says the ship is nearly 20 years old and that she can do a maximum of 15 knots, but she usually only does 13 to save fuel. He says we'll have lost about three hours so we'll have two hours ashore wherever we're going instead of five.'

'Lucky to get there at all,' said Grandpa. 'I

suppose this friend of yours didn't say where we were bound *for*?'

'No. I did ask, but he said it wouldn't be a Mystery Tour if we knew. His name is Mr. McFarlane and he says he'd like to meet you if there's time.'

'I shan't be going far,' said Grandpa and he settled down to do the crossword. He was really quite glad of the rest as he'd been working extremely hard as a relief handyman on a small holiday camp which had meant very long hours although the money had been good.

'P'raps it's time we settled down a bit,' Grandpa thought to himself, chewing the stem of his pipe. 'Ah well, something'll come along.'

What did come along as they once more surged out into the misty sea was Billy's new acquaintance, Mr. McFarlane, the ship's assistant engineer who, like Billy, was liberally covered in black oil. He was a small man, not much taller than Billy and he looked like a worried monkey.

'Well now,' he said, 'is your Grandpa about?'

'Gone to sleep again.'

'I see.'

Mr. McFarlane scowled so much his black eyebrows met in the middle. He looked from Grandpa, now fast out with his mouth open and his pipe lying on his chest to Ben underneath the bench. Both of them were snoring steadily and in chorus.

'I'm afraid I've got some bad news for you,' Mr. McFarlane said abruptly. 'You seem a sensible sort of boy so I'll tell you direct. It's about that dog of yours.'

Billy felt a horrible sinking sensation in his middle. Ben looked perfectly OK and as Billy very well knew he hadn't left Grandpa's side since they'd come on board so he couldn't have done anything awful. Anyway, Ben was a very peaceable sort of dog.

'Usually we advise against passengers bringing their dogs on board, but there's a temporary girl in the booking office at the moment and she doesn't know all the wrinkles of the job.'

'Yes,' said Billy in a voice which didn't sound at all like his own.

'Because sometimes we do have a little setback,' went on Mr. McFarlane scowling horribly at the flat, pale blue sea. He was obviously hating what he had to say and Billy's stomach went down another couple of notches. 'Like today. The Captain had no chance to do anything but make for the nearest port and I'm afraid it's your hard luck that it happened to be a French one. Darn fool regulations, but you can't get away from it, so that's that.'

'What?'

'That dog of yours. It'll have to go into quarantine for six months once we get back to the mainland.'

Mr. McFarlane spoke with a rush, but Billy,

usually a quick witted boy, just couldn't take the words in and he just stared blankly at the engineer who now looked absolutely fruious.

'I know it's unfair and stupid, or so it seems to us, but it's because of the rabies you see. You know that's the illness that dogs can catch and which if they *do* get it and they bite you, well, you die. There's rabies, not much but a little, on the Continent, but there's none in Britain. It's been kept out by the very strict laws on pets and I'm afraid that dog of yours has broken the law.'

'But he hasn't *been* ashore. He's never been off the ship,' Billy burst out. He was still only taking in part of what Mr. McFarlane was telling him, but it was starting to make horrible sense.

'Ah, but *technically* you and your dog *have* been to France, according to the letter of the law that is. I'm sorry, son, I really am, but there's not a thing you, nor me, nor your Grandpa, nor I daresay the Queen of England herself can do about it. That there dog will have to go into quarantine for six months and that's that!'

Mr. McFarlane put his hand on Billy's shoulder for a moment and then went swinging off down the deck leaving Billy staring after him. He still couldn't take it all in, but all the excitement and happiness had gone out of the day. How on earth was he going to break the news to Grandpa? Grandpa and Ben hadn't been parted for a day, let alone six months, since they had met through the netting of the Dogs Home when Ben was a puppy and looked rather like a feather duster. Wherever Grandpa went then Ben would go too. Grandpa had even turned down some good jobs because there had been a 'No Dogs' rule attached to the work.

Billy looked at the two sleeping faces which somehow seemed rather alike. Ben wasn't a young dog any more, in fact he was decidedly elderly. He would be really miserable in some rotten old dog place. He would mope and fret and scratch himself and he might even die of homesickness. As for what it would do to Grandpa . . . Billy clamped his teeth together and screwed his eyes up so tightly that he could see little burning stars. What *was* he going to do? What *could* he do? Everything kept going round and round in his mind while the two snorers peacefully slept on.

Billy was still leaning miserably against the rail staring ahead without really seeing anything when the mist eddied and whirled and started to break up a little. Billy watched it without much interest. He didn't even care about where they were headed. He just wished they had never seen the rotten notice and never come on board the rotten boat or stopped off at the rotten French port. Above his head the ship's hooter suddenly let out a long 'Toooooot-Toooooot' and the engine room bell rang. Grandpa and Ben stirred and their snoring stopped and Billy went on gazing ahead, trying to brace himself for the awful moment when he would have to tell Grandpa about Ben.

And then a very strange thing happened. With a flurry the mist curled away as though an unseen hand had drawn aside a filmy curtain and there, straight ahead of Billy, was land. It was difficult to say how far away it was, because distances are always tricky to judge at sea, especially when there's mist lying on the surface of the water. But it was land right enough, with light green grass growing up a large hill which was covered in yellow bushes. And it wasn't just the unexpectedness of the land appearing, it was what was on it that made Billy forget all his troubles for a moment. There, jutting out from the rocky foreshore, was a castle which seemed to be floating on the sea. A proper old-fashioned castle with one turret which was leaning away from the main building at an angle, and beyond that and closer to the shore was another smaller cone-shaped turret which vanished behind the first turret as the ship chugged past. And beyond that again was a great fortress wall.

Billy stared at the odd, jumbled shape of the castle. It was like nothing he had ever seen before in his life. There was something very strange about it, but what that strangeness was he didn't know and then, as abruptly as it had appeared, it disappeared. The

misty curtains swept back into place and it was as if he had imagined the whole thing.

'Excuse me,' Billy said to a passenger who had come to lean on the rail nearby – it was the man who liked to look on the gloomy side of things – 'did you see that castle?'

'Castle, what castle? I didn't see any castle. I shall be glad to see the harbour and get ashore for a bit. If you ask me, we should get half our money back for the way we've been treated. Castle, indeed!'

He stumped off and Grandpa, with Ben at his heels, came over and looked at Billy.

'What's the matter with you then?' he asked. 'You look as if you've lost a pound and found a penny. Hallo, here comes land now if I'm not much mistaken. What do you think of that, old fellow?'

Ben went 'Hm hm' and wagged his tail.

It was at that moment that Billy, his head whirling with quarantine regulations and mysterious castles, made up his mind that somehow, by some desperate means, he was going to save Ben. Although how, where or when he hadn't the faintest idea.

3 · The Runaways

At any other time Billy would really have enjoyed arriving at their mysterious destination. Everybody was now crowding up against the rails, the ship's siren was telling the harbour that they were arriving and the mist at last began to burn off faster and faster so that they could see exactly where they were heading. There was a long, curving, sandy bay with a great rocky headland at the far end into which was built what appeared to be an enormous fort. There were palm trees and a big grassy shelf of land with some small white houses tucked away in a dip, and closer to a line of houses which followed the line of the bay. The harbour wall was very long, pointing out into the sea like a great finger and at its land end were small warehouses and a row of tall, thin houses with pointed red roofs.

'Ah, I know where this is,' said the gloomy man, 'I came here years ago and I didn't care for it then. If you ask me they should have told us where we were going and then I wouldn't have come.'

'Why's that, then?' asked Grandpa.

'Nothing to do. Few hotels, few shops, some

broken down old forts. The roads aren't properly made up, just cobbles that are hard on your feet. If you ask me . . .'

'What's it called?' asked Billy.

He had almost, but not quite forgotten the trouble with Ben for a minute, because as the ship came round the end of the harbour wall and began to sail towards the quay with the view changing all the time, Billy felt as though he was being pulled towards this unknown place. It was as if in some weird way he knew it already.

'It's called Riduna. It's only a rocky little island. Terrible currents they have round here too. *I* shouldn't care to go here in the winter. It must be a dead and alive place then. It'd be about eight miles to the east of Le Huquet and sixty miles south of England. Something of that nature.'

'It doesn't look too bad to me,' said Grandpa, giving Billy the ghost of a wink. 'Pity we shan't be able to stay longer. I'd like to have had a look round and Ben'll need to stretch his legs. What's the matter with you Billy? Not sea sick are you?'

Billy shook his head. He didn't want to talk because he might blurt out the news about Ben. He just wanted to get ashore to try and sort things out.

The ship edged in, going more and more slowly until she was hardly moving as they came alongside the quay. Ropes were thrown, the sea stopped churning under their bows and the engine room bell rang as, with a final 'toooooot', they came to a halt. Although the sea had been exceptionally calm, it felt odd being on solid ground again because it was as though it was tilting slowly up and down. Mr. McFarlane was down on the quay directing the unloading of the cargo as a crane moved up alongside and its great claws came down to grip hold of a crate. Billy would quite like to have watched how it was done if things had been ordinary, but now he only wanted to get away before Mr. McFarlane had a chance to speak to Grandpa. Billy thought he had got away with it, but a voice called after them.

'Don't forget now, back on board by 4.50 sharp for sailing at 5.'

'Aye, aye,' said Grandpa, who was still being a sailor with the hold-alls up on his shoulder.

'Let's go and find somewhere to eat,' Billy gabbled.

'Food, food, all you think about is food.'

Actually Billy didn't feel all that hungry for once as he was too worried and anxious, but when they found a small café tucked away in the row of tall houses, the delicious smells made him feel a little better. Ben, who had been zig-zagging backwards and forwards across the cobbles with his tail going like a furious mop, would have preferred to have gone on exploring, but they finally persuaded him inside.

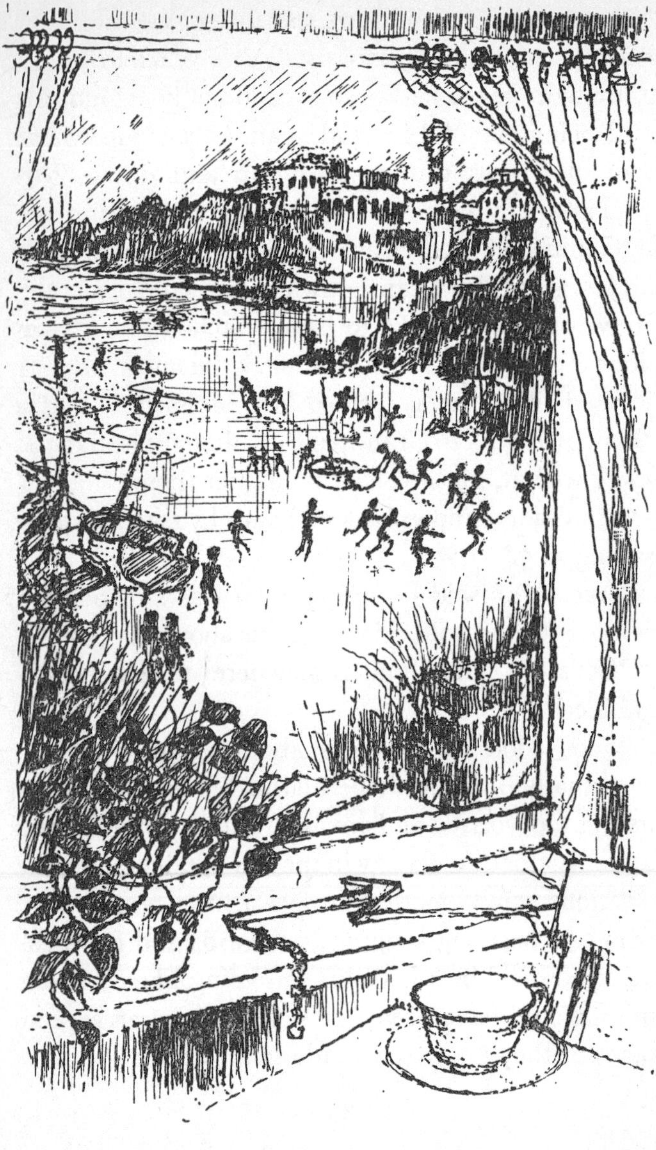

'Well then, eh,' said the woman who ran the café. 'You'll be late for your meal, but I heard you had trouble with your engines. It's a good thing its so still today. The bass is fresh caught last night, you try that.'

She gave them a table by the big window which looked out across the sandy bay. It was a good quarter of a mile long with some small rocks in the middle, a jetty over on the harbour side with two very sturdy, but old-fashioned looking fishing boats tied up to it. As it was half tide they had come to rest on the sand and were tilted over. There were men digging for bait, some children playing cricket, a number of yachts and through a slight dip between the big fort at the far end of the bay and the small tucked away houses, Billy could just see the top of the lighthouse. Because it was such a hazy day its brilliant white light was working and sending out flashes every few seconds. It was all very interesting, but what surprised both Grandpa and Billy was that there weren't more people about. They had got so used to crowds. Grandpa asked the woman about it when she brought the fish.

'Bless you, this *is* crowded!' she said laughing. 'Why, there must be fifty people down on the sands. All the other beaches will be about the same. There aren't no big hotels here or amusement parks and such like so the people who come here are the ones who like things a bit more simple. Make your own fun.'

Billy ate steadily while Ben watched him – or appeared to watch him; you never could tell if he was actually looking at you or not through the thick fringe of fur he wore over his eyes – with his shaggy head leaning warmly against Billy's knee. More and more the weird feeling was creeping over Billy that he knew this place quite well. It was as if he had dreamt about it, or imagined it, or seen it in a picture. But he just couldn't think where.

'Staying long?' the woman asked as she came to clear away their empty plates.

'No, we're going back on the boat,' Grandpa said regretfully.

'Don't miss her, now,' the woman said, laughing. 'There was an elderly couple did that a fortnight ago. Went to sleep on the beach and woke up to see her steaming past. A real state they were in, but they made the best of it in the end and I put them up here and they had a nice little holiday.'

The vague beginnings of a plan began to form in the back of Billy's mind. He stared out of the window while his ice cream melted on the plate in front of him.

'Pity we've only got a couple of hours here,' Grandpa said, sticking his empty pipe into the corner of his mouth, 'it's got a good smell to it, this place.

Different. Well now we are here we'd better have a look round. We'll leave our luggage here.'

The woman stowed it away and gave them a map so that they could find their way up into town. It was quite a steep climb up a twisting road and although Grandpa was very fit for his age, he was puffing away by the time they reached the shops. They bought a bowl with a map of the island on it for Ben, a very dashing sailing cap for Grandpa and a blue T-shirt for Billy with 'I'VE BEEN TO RIDUNA' on it.

'Think I'll just rest my legs a bit,' Grandpa said, spotting a café with tables and chairs outside on the pavement, 'and watch the world go by.'

'And I'll take Ben for a walk,' said Billy.

He felt both excited and sick at the same time because he knew, more or less now, what he was going to do.

'Not too far now,' said Grandpa.

'OK,' said Billy, crossing his fingers behind his back.

They set off down a small cobbled side road where Ben would keep stopping to sniff at walls and doorways. Billy let him off the lead because there was hardly any traffic and what there was travelled very slowly because of the cobbles. Nothing seemed to move very fast, even the people were dawdling along and stopping to talk to each other and several complete strangers smiled at Billy; one small woman with a rather cross looking girl actually said that Ben looked like a darling.

Ben didn't seem to mind and he waved his tail and allowed the woman to stroke him about where his ears were. Billy was bit alarmed that she might start asking questions so he urged Ben on and round the corner where they came face to face with another very steep road and a pair of gateways which had a notice outside that read: 'Riduna Animal Welfare. Tuesday Market Now Open.' Billy thought it was a funny way to sell animals, but then everything about this small island seemed unusual and, for the moment, all he wanted to do was to find somewhere he and Ben could hide out. Because the idea had really set in his mind now. They were going to run away and miss the boat. That would give him another seven days in which to think of some way to save Ben and perhaps, with any luck, Mr. McFarlane wouldn't be on board and Grandpa might never find out about the quarantine rules. If only he could find the vanishing castle he was sure they would be safe there, but he hadn't been able to work out where it was on the map and he didn't want to ask anybody because that would only draw attention to them.

The trouble was that people noticed Ben anyway, he was that kind of dog with his amiable face and large feet, so Billy made for the countryside and they were soon away from the small, softly coloured houses and onto an earth track which led to the cliffs. Sky larks hung singing in the pale blue sky and a covey of partridges put up by Ben went scurrying off as fast as their little legs would carry them. A rabbit skipped away almost from under their feet and a bull turned and looked at them. Billy made a grab for Ben as the bull, which looked extremely large and none too friendly, had only a rather frayed rope round its wide neck. One good toss of its head would surely either snap the tether or bring the small stake to which it was attached straight out of the ground.

'Hm hm hm,' said Ben, who had never before been so close to a bull. The bull put down its enormous head and glared at them with little red eyes.

'Sh, Ben, good boy,' said Billy very softly. 'We'll just walk on quietly.'

Ben seemed to understand that this was not the moment to try and get on friendly terms with another animal and he plodded along at Billy's heels until the path took another turning and the bull was out of sight.

'Well done,' said Billy, whose heart was beating very rapidly.

They had reached the edge of some high cliffs by now and the grass was bumpy with mole hills and covered in yellow broom bushes which filled the warm air with a very sweet smell. There was a continual deep buzzing which came from hundreds of bees, some of them large and yellow and black, others which were smaller and a reddy-brown in colour. A very large and shiny stag beetle with long, curving horns plodded across the dusty path and Billy bent down and picked it up carefully. It didn't seem to mind but just went on walking up his arm until it reached his shoulder where it stopped. So Billy let it stay there and it began to preen and clean itself as Billy walked on looking as if he had a shiny black brooch on his T-shirt.

There was such a lot to see and examine, because there was wildlife everywhere, but Billy was intent on finding somewhere they could hide. The island might be quite small, but the little coastal path went in and out so much that it was about three miles further on that Billy spotted the perfect hiding place.

It was a very old barn made of boulders. It was tucked away in the side of the hill and it smelt of corn and earth. It obviously hadn't been used for years and the door was only hanging on one hinge. Billy gave it a push and it opened slowly showing a shadowy interior. It was at times like this that it was a great help having Ben along. He put his whiskery face round the door, sniffed and then waved his tail as he turned and licked Billy's hand.

'We'll just stay here until the boat goes,' Billy explained. 'Better make ourselves comfortable. It's lucky I've got some sweets with me or we might get

hungry. Cripes, I hope Grandpa doesn't get too furious. . .'

He and Ben shared the sweets, leaning their backs against some old grain sacks which had split long ago so that the grain had run all over the floor. It looked as if rabbits and partridges and probably field mice had discovered this treasure as there were small trails of it in all directions.

The beetle, perhaps feeling that it had travelled far enough, plodded down Billy's arm then his leg and finally negotiated his ankle like an elderly man climbing down a steep step. Once on the earth floor it did a bit more cleaning up of its shining shell and then set off for the outside world in its determined way.

Billy yawned so Ben did the same. Perhaps it was the heat, or the excitements and upsets of the day and the sea journey or the long walk, or perhaps it was everything put together, because Billy's eyelids got heavier and heavier until he could no longer keep them open. Then Ben started to snore, blowing out his grey and white moustache with every breath, and that steady, comforting noise made Billy's head jerk forward.

'As soon as the boat goes we'll walk back to Grandpa,' he said and a minute after that he was sound asleep.

Down at the harbour the boat's warning siren

called and called, sending the seagulls whirling up into the sky. But although the sound travelled across the island it didn't make either of the two fugatives budge an inch. They were both of them dead to the world and in Ben's case, judging by the way he twitched from time to time, having a wonderful dream in which he was a young puppy again and chasing rabbits.

4 · 'Owwwww'

It was dark when Billy woke up and for a moment he couldn't think where he was and then he hardly dared to breathe because quite close at hand and getting closer by the second, was the most extraordinary noise. Part snuffle and part grunt, it sounded as though a large and bad tempered animal was advancing towards him. Billy screwed up his eyes and as they got used to the darkness he was able to see the outline of the half open door and beyond that, soft moonlight. He put out his hand for the comforting warm roughness of Ben's coat, but there was nothing there.

'Ben,' Billy said in a hoarse whisper, 'Ben!'

The snuffling animal didn't seem to hear him for it kept advancing, but although Billy looked and looked, he *couldn't see it*. His heart was thundering and although it was a warm, still night his hands and feet and the back of his neck all felt cold. He would have given anything to be on board the boat with Grandpa telling him off, but as it was he was trapped miles from anywhere and nobody knew where he was and Ben had gone missing. He was old and he didn't always look where he was going . . . he might have fallen over the cliff.

Billy forgot all about his own troubles and fears and rolled over onto his knees and it was then that he saw the animal which was making all the noise. It was just inside the doorway and it was muttering and snuffling to iself as if it was grumbling under its breath. In fact for its size it was making a tremendous amount of noise. It was about as long as Billy's foot, it had a round body, a sniffling little snout and very small eyes.

'A hedgehog!' said Billy and put out his hand to pick it up. It immediately rolled itself up very tightly and stopped snorting. The prickles weren't sharp enough to hurt as Billy held it gently, but the little animal, which was pale grey in the moonlight, only unwound itself slightly to show the end of its pointed snout so Billy put it down again.

No sooner had he got his breath back over that when the most awful sound suddenly broke out. It was like a loud moaning cry which rose to a howl. Slowly Billy put his head round the door, half expecting to see some ghastly spirit flying through the night sky, but instead there was Ben perched on the top of a flat rock and baying at the moon,

'Owwwwww,' he sang, 'Owwwwwww.'

'You idiot,' Billy scowled at him, 'giving me a fright.'

'Owwwwww.'

Billy put his arms round him and Ben turned and leant his large head against Billy's shoulder and gave a deep, contented sigh.

'Well, we've missed the boat all right,' Billy said.

The pair of them sat side by side staring out across the dark, rippling sea where the lights of the fishing boats bobbed up and down while much further out on the horizon, a big oil tanker moved slowly through the moon's path. It was very peaceful; although the night was full of soft noises and Billy knew he ought to be worrying about getting back to Grandpa, he didn't feel as if he wanted to move.

He must have fallen asleep again lying against Ben, because the next thing he knew was that there was a noise like a sawmill going full blast some where out to sea, a cock was crowing and two enormous gulls, flying side by side with their necks outstretched, were calling to each other at the tops of their voices. It was quite light by now and the sun was climbing up through the mist which was lying on the sea like a lumpy bedspread. Billy realised all this in a vague sort of way, but what was far more important was that he was so hungry his stomach was making more noise than everything else put together. Ben seemed to be feeling the same because he put his grey muzzle up against Billy's face and moaned deep in his throat, 'Hm hm hm.'

'We'd better get back,' Billy said.

He got up and shook his head and looked around for the path they had taken yesterday. It went quite close to the edge of the cliffs and when he looked over the edge he saw where the sawmill sound was coming from. Far, far below was a great, jagged rock absolutely covered in birds and floating round and round it on enormous, spread wings were perhaps two hundred more birds all making this ugly grating noise. It seemed to be getting louder and louder and then Billy realised that the noise was coming from behind him as well. He turned round just in time to see a small Police van bumping across the grass towards him.

'Oh, *cripes*!' said Billy.

He didn't recognise the driver, but the other head with its thatch of white hair he knew only too well. Grandpa leapt out of the van before it had even stopped and before Billy knew quite what was happening, Grandpa had gripped him by the scruff of his anorak and was shaking him so hard that he was dancing backwards and forwards on his toes. Everything seemed to be happening at once.

'And *where* have you been?' Grandpa demanded.

'Wha-wha-what . . .'

'Whoooooof.'

Ben let out one of his rare deep lion like roars and padded round and round them.

'Now then, sir,' said the policeman, half in and half out of the van as Ben was now advancing towards him showing all his elderly yellow teeth.

'Come along, answer me *at once*!'

'Wha-wha-wha . . .'

'Whoooooof!'

Grandpa let go just as suddenly as he had pounced and Billy sat down with a thud on the springy grass. Both of them were very out of breath.

'You all right?' Grandpa asked anxiously.

Billy nodded, which made his head spin more than ever. The policeman, who had managed to persuade Ben that he was a friend, came over to them and went 'Tck tck tck.' He was a big man with fairish hair and a moustache and he put his hand up over his mouth as though he was trying to hide a smile.

'A fair old time you've given us,' he said, 'there's your Grandfather thinking you've been kidnapped. Although we haven't had a case of that since some pirates sailing in here about three hundred years ago and even then the lad was got back with no harm done, or so the story goes.'

Everybody had quietened down by the time he'd finished speaking and Billy muttered.

'I'm sorry, Grandpa. I knew you'd be worried, but . . .'

'Worried? *Worried?* You're old enough and ugly enough to look after yourself. But it's why you did it

that muddles me. Of *course* I wasn't really worried.
Well?'

Billy's stomach gave an extra loud rumble and the
policeman bent down and stroked Ben who immediately leant heavily against his legs as though his own
were too tired to support him.

'Perhaps we'd better get back into town,' said the
policeman. 'And all this can be sorted out over some
breakfast. The café'll be open down by the harbour
because of the fishing boats coming in.'

'Hm,' said Grandpa, sounding like Ben, 'all right
then, but I mean to get the truth out of you, Billy, so
don't you try and wriggle away from it.'

It was quite a bouncy ride back to town during
which Billy desperately tried to think of some
explanation before they reached the harbour. The
policeman seemed okay, but he could hardly admit in
front of him that he wanted to break the law over Ben.
Perhaps he would go away, Billy thought hopefully.
But there was no such luck, the policeman stuck like
glue. He stopped the blue van opposite the café, and
went over and held the door open so that Billy had to
get out, and as he glanced up he saw that although
the policeman still had a twinkle in his eye, he also
looked very determined. Billy's heart went down
another couple of notches.

The woman, who had served them lunch
yesterday, just nodded and returned in a very short

time with three plates full of bacon and egg and sausage and potato cakes. There was also tea and toast and honey. Nobody spoke as they were all too busy eating.

But once their empty plates had been taken away and Grandpa had clamped his pipe between his teeth, Billy knew that the dreaded moment had come and there was no way out. However, rather to his suprise, Grandpa was the one who now seemed to be nervous. He glared at the table top and then out of the window and then at the pipe as though he'd never seen it before.

'Well now,' he said, 'when you and Ben ran away yesterday and the boat had to sail without us – my word that was a to do – I went to the Police Station and met Constable Martin here. We went all over the place looking for you, there was a search party out and even talk of bringing in a helicopter from France.'

'Sorry,' mumbled Billy.

'We didn't think you'd come to much harm,' the policeman said, 'not with the two of you being together. I'm very sorry about your dog, Billy.'

Billy clutched at Ben's thick fur and stared. He knew at that moment that the policeman knew about the quarantine law and that in a second Grandpa was going to hear the horrible truth, and there was nothing he could do to stop it.

Billy began to scowl just as much as Grandpa and although nearly fifty years separated them in age they looked very alike as both of them stared at the policeman who cleared his throat and said in a very official sounding voice.

'It's my duty to tell you that owing to official instructions with regard to the quarantine laws that . . .'

'It's all right,' said Grandpa, 'you don't have to go through all that rigmarole. I know about it. The long and the short is, Billy, that Ben's got to go into Kennels for six months.'

'I know.'

'It's all part of some daft law because we . . . You *know*?'

'Yes, that's why we missed the boat. I thought . . .'

There was another long silence during which PC Martin crossed his arms and tilted back his chair and stared out across the sands to where a couple of fishermen were digging for bait and a rather cross looking girl was plodding along with a bucket and a shrimping net.

'Well, it can't be helped,' said Granpa. 'It looks as if we're stuck here for a month until the boat comes in again, and how we'll manage or what we'll do, dear knows. While as to what we do about Ben . . .'

'Ah now that *is* a problem,' PC Martin agreed. All three of them looked at Ben who got embarrassed and wriggled further backwards under the table. Billy shut his eyes and thought so hard his face went bright red and as if out of nowhere two words flashed into his mind and he said them aloud.

'Animal Welfare.'

'We've all got that in mind, lad,' said PC Martin. 'Oh, you mean the Animal Shelter up at the top of town. Well, they do take in strays.'

'Ben's hardly a stray,' Grandpa said huffily.

But Billy had already dived under the table and was hauling out a protesting Ben. Although it was usually Grandpa who did the talking now it was Billy's turn and he just kept on and on until all four of them were bundled back into the van and driving up the steep hill.

'Now don't you get too carried away,' said PC Martin when he at last managed to get a word in. 'It may be that Ben'll have to be sent back to the mainland somehow or . . .' He didn't say or what and Grandpa suddenly got very busy pushing Ben out of the van.

The Animal Welfare turned out to be a muddled sort of collection of small buildings round a central courtyard. A very large tabby cat without a tail stalked past them and an enormous red and green macaw walked sideways down a tree and snapped his beak while from one of the buildings came barks, mews and a prolonged bleat. This last noise was explained when a door flew open and a goat emerged dragging behind it a girl in a white overall.

'With you in a minute,' she said breathlessly as they trotted past. 'Could you wait over there . . .'

They sat round stiffly in the waiting room which had posters on the wall about how to look after pets and a particularly nasty one which was a warning about rabies. Grandpa and Billy both avoided looking at it and Constable Martin stared straight ahead in his usual way. Ben lay under the table and complained at the back of his throat. He knew quite well that something was going on which concerned him and it made him uneasy.

The little nurse came bouncing back a few minutes later and Grandpa and the policeman took it in turns to tell her what had happened.

'Oh I see,' she said at the end, 'it does seem unfair when Ben didn't even land in France, but it's the law and we have to stick to it. About a year ago a small private plane was diverted and the same thing happened. In that case the gentleman and his dog were very upset and there was quite a stir about it in the newspapers and on television, but the dog had to go into quarantine just the same.'

'But couldn't *you* take Ben?' Billy burst out, unable to keep quiet any longer.

'Yes we can, just. After that last case the committee decided that we should have a separate kennel in

case it ever happened again. And you'd be able to come and see him every day.'

Billy could have sunk through the floor with relief.

'How long is quarantine?' asked Grandpa.

'Six months.'

'It'll soon pass,' said the policeman helpfully, although to Billy it sounded like a lifetime.

'Yes, I daresay,' agreed Grandpa, 'but there is one slight snag. If Ben's *here* for six months then Billy and me'll have to be here too and how are we going to manage *that*?'

5 · Grandpa Gets A Job

'Something'll come along, you'll see,' said Billy.

'That's what *I* say, not you,' said Grandpa.

They were sitting on a grass bank at the front of the Animal Welfare with Ben between them. Above their heads the macaw, who was called Winston and was very short tempered with strangers, edged down the tree and said hoarsely.

'Clear off. Hop it. Go on.'

Billy put his chin on his knees and thought so hard he felt as if his head might blow up. Even to Grandpa he couldn't say how much he liked this strange island which looked as if it had half a hundred places to explore and discover. Cliffs and caves, bays and boulders, forts and castles. Especially that mysterious castle he had glimpsed for a moment through the sea mist; he was quite sure it *had* been there even though the Gloomy Man had said he hadn't seen it. He wanted to stay here with Grandpa and Ben more than he had ever wanted anything before in his life.

'Even supposing I *could* get a job,' Grandpa went on, 'we'd have nowhere to stay and as it's the start of the summer season it stands to reason that it would cost a lot to live in a guest house. It doesn't look as if there are any big firms here where they'd have places for us to stay. And come to that, I don't suppose the wages are all that high. It's a puzzle.'

'Clear off!' shouted Winston.

Ben, who knew very well that Grandpa and Billy were worried, lost his usual calm manner and put back his shaggy head and roared.

'Whooooof.'

Winston scuttled up to the top of the tree as if his tail feathers had been tweaked and then shut his eyes and pretended he had become invisible. Ben subsided.

'I don't think there's anything for it, Billy. We'll have to go back to the mainland. Perhaps we'll find some work near a kennels there.'

Billy's mouth went down at the corners and Grandpa went on hastily.

'And no more running away, mind. That never solves anything.'

'We could at least *ask* about work. Perhaps they might want somebody here.'

Billy was desperate enough to try anything and as he bounded back into the building Constable Martin, who had been listening to his radio, said, 'Well, I give him 'A' for trying. If you hold on a moment I'll have a word with the lighthouse.'

'I couldn't do that sort of work. I'm not trained for it,' Grandpa said, looking rather startled.

'No, it's not that. It's just that up the lighthouse they know most things which are going on around the island.'

And he began to murmur away into his radio. Billy was talking to the nurse who was going round feeding all the animals who were being looked after while their owners were away. There were several cats, four small black and white kittens all bunched together with their stubby little tails stuck up in the air, a large tortoise which looked about a thousand years old, an elderly black labrador with red rimmed eyes and a sad expression, an elegant white poodle, five budgerigars all talking at once and at the very end of the corridor two pointed black ears which just showed above the wire netting.

'No, I *am* sorry,' the nurse said, stopping to stroke one of the cats, a very beautiful grey tabby with round yellow eyes who was going mad with delight. 'We only have a vet, who comes over once a week from one of the other islands, and me. Then there are the two ladies who run the market, but they don't get paid. So I'm afraid there wouldn't be any work for your grandpa here. Do you like animals?'

'I don't know much about them,' said Billy, tickling the grey cat under the chin at which it began to purr even more loudly, 'except for Ben that is and I like him all right. He'd *hate* being shut away in some old dogs' home with people he didn't know.'

'He'd be shut away if he came here.'

'Yes, but Grandpa and I could see him every day so he wouldn't get lonely and you wouldn't be cruel to him.'

'I should hope not,' the nurse said laughing, and then she began feeding the budgerigars so she didn't have to look at Billy, because she *had* heard of animal homes where the animals did live in very bad conditions, so bad that sometimes they died of disease or starvation.

'Last one,' she said, arriving at the end door where the two black ears were. She opened it up and a very young dog with a short black and white coat came bounding out to meet them. She had bright eyes, a whippy tail, and she had some trouble not running over her own feet which somehow seemed too large for her.

'And this is Boddie, short for Bodecia – awful name to give a little dog isn't it? But she belonged to an old lady who died suddenly so Boddie has to come and live here until someone else adopts her. She answers to her name now so she's stuck with it. Boddie, this is Billy.'

Boddie butted him in the knees, turned round three times, fell over her feet and collapsed with her legs crossed in all directions.

'What she needs is exercise,' said the nurse. 'I take her out as often as I can, but there's not a lot of time.'

'I'd take her,' said Billy and stopped.

'But first your grandpa needs a job and you need somewhere to live. I know. It was a bit like that when I first came here and the Welfare was just a lot of old farm buildings. I hadn't got anywhere to go either while the builders were in, but it didn't matter really as it was summer time so I lived in a tent down on the camping site. All right, Boddie, that's enough. I'll take you onto the beach this evening.'

Boddie went over backwards with her ears up and then whined in the back of her throat as the nurse shut the door.

'We haven't got a tent,' Billy said, trailing along behind the nurse.

'Oh, that's no problem. You can hire one quite cheaply.'

Billy wondered what 'cheap' meant. At one of the schools he'd been to, a boy had said that five pounds was cheap for a pen, but to Billy that had seemed a great deal of money. He walked out into the sunshine where Grandpa was talking softly to Ben.

'It wasn't anybody's fault, old chap. It was just hard luck. We'll find you the best home we possibly can and we'll visit you often.' Ben shook his head and whined 'Hm hm' on a high note. 'You and I'll make the best of it, but young Billy's going to take it badly.

64

Well he's known you all his life so it stand to . . . hallo, Billy. Just telling Ben what a fine day it is. Funny sort of island this, isn't it?'

'Um. From the boat I saw . . .' said Billy and stopped. No, he still couldn't even tell Grandpa about the mysterious vanishing castle. If only they could stay here in this strange place and be near Ben and he could find the castle everything would be perfect.

'I don't want to worry you,' said the nurse as she came out of the Welfare to join them in the sunshine, 'but I've just been talking to our vet, Mr. Peter, and he says that Ben will have to go into the isolation kennel right away. Either here or over on the mainland.'

'But how can we *get* to the mainland?' asked Grandpa.

'By chartering a boat. It will cost rather a lot I'm afraid, but there's nothing else you *can* do. Unless . . .' The nurse glanced at Ben who was lying full out in the shade with his whiskers blowing up and down in time to his snores. Billy didn't understand what she meant for a moment and then he glanced at Grandpa who had gone quite white underneath his tan so that he looked awful. Quite old for once and blotchy.

'I couldn't,' said Grandpa in an uneven voice, 'not *Ben*. I would if he was too old or in pain, but not now he's still enjoying himself. He's one of the family, you see.'

'What do you mean?' Billy asked, looking from the nurse to Grandpa to Ben. 'Do what? You mean *kill* him!'

There was silence apart from all the sounds which the animals were making. Billy wanted to say something, but he felt as if all the breath had been smothered out of him and then there was the crunch of gravel and Constable Martin came up the drive putting his radio back in his shirt pocket.

'Clear off,' shouted Winston from the top of his tree.

'Well then,' said the policeman, 'I've had a word with the lighthouse and the keeper on duty says he's heard that old Fred Quevain, you'll know Fred, Briony?'

'That's right. Got a lovely basset and works up at the Grand Harbour Hotel,' said the nurse while Billy wondered for a moment if the basset worked there or its master.

'Ah, that's the point,' said Constable Martin. 'Fred's just handed in his notice. His daughter's over from Australia and he wants to have time to spend with her and to put out his pots.'

By now Grandpa looked as flummoxed as Billy, but at least nobody was talking about death any more.

'Just like an islander!' Constable Martin went on,

'the moment it's good fishing weather it's down tools and get the boat out. Well Fred's job's there if you're interested.'

'What sort of job is it?' Grandpa and Billy asked together.

'Sort of general handyman. Anything from cleaning the windows to carrying the luggage and giving a hand behind the bar. Don't suppose the pay'll be too grand, but there'll be tips.'

'Well,' said Grandpa, 'I'll take any sort of work, that's no worry, but would there be accommodation with it? Billy and me can't sleep on the beach. At least not for more'n a couple of nights.'

'Not as far as I know,' said the policeman. 'There'll be chalets for the regular staff, but Fred's got his own house nearby.'

'We could sleep out for a couple of nights,' Billy said hoarsely. 'And then something'll come along. It's *bound* to. Or . . .' And the answer came out of nowhere again in the same extraordinary way it had before.

'Or?' said the other three like a chorus.

'There's the camping site,' Billy gabbled, 'We could hire a tent and live in that and I shouldn't think it would cost much. Oh do say yes, Grandpa, do. Think of Ben.'

Ben suddenly shook himself and went bounding off barking furiously. Everybody had been listening so hard to what was going on that they hadn't noticed that Winston had come sideways down the tree and was now rolling towards them, rocking from side to side with his neck stuck forward.

'ARRRRRUMPH,' went Ben.

Winston quite literally left the ground about six inches and then made for the nearest tree which he shot up like a squirel while Ben barked round and round the trunk.

'Clear off! Hop it!' shrieked Winston, jerking his head backwards and forwards. 'You're not wanted. Go on.'

It was a wonderful sight, but Billy hardly noticed. All his attention was fixed on Grandpa, who stuck his empty pipe into the corner of his mouth, shifted his spectacles to the top of his head, frowned horribly and said.

'Living in a tent at *my* age? I ask you! Oh, all right, all right, I agree. But I haven't got the job yet mind, so don't go getting too airy fairy about it.'

'Oh yes you have,' said Constable Martin, 'I took the liberty of asking the lighthouse keeper to put through a call to the Grand Harbour saying you'd be coming over. I hope you don't object?'

But for once both Grandpa and Billy were past speech so it was left to Ben to have the last word as he collapsed in an exhausted heap underneath the tree:

'ERRRRUMPH. HM HM.'

6 · Camping out

The Grand Harbour turned out to be not quite as grand as its name. It was a longish, low, white building high above the harbour so that there was a wonderful view of the sea and the coastline where Billy's quick eyes picked out no fewer than three old forts, but none of them looked quite right for his mysterious castle. Or that could have been because he was looking at them sideways on and there was no mist about, only a sparkling blue sea. There was a cricket pitch quite close to the hotel and Billy reckoned that if you hit a really good six it would go clear over the edge of the field and fall not far short of the harbour down below. There was a tennis court on which four rather large ladies were playing and the thud of a spring board and the splash of water showed that there was a swimming pool at the back of the hotel.

'Mr. Er?' said a man with curly hair and very bright blue eyes, bouncing out of the main entrance yards before they reached it.

'Luft,' said Grandpa, putting down the luggage to shake hands.

'And I'm Roy Parker. I own the hotel. They told me at the lighthouse that you'd be along. I gather you're looking for a job. Come into the office. And this is?'

'My grandson Billy.'

Billy found his hand being shaken very fast and then they were whisked through the foyer and into a small room where there were two desks, mounds of papers and a pretty girl with long blonde hair talking on a telephone.

'Tell 'em I'm out whoever it is,' said Mr. Parker sitting down on his swivel chair and making it spin round. He was one of the fastest people Billy had ever seen and he made it seem as if everybody else was moving at half speed. He rattled off a lot of questions which Grandpa answered and at the end of about ten minutes, Mr. Parker glanced at his watch and said,

'I'm sure you could do the job all right, Mr. Luft. I'll have a word with the States about getting you a work permit.'

'*The States!*' said Grandpa, 'I've never worked in America.'

'No, no,' said Mr. Parker, giving a couple of spins on his chair, 'the States are like our local government office. I'm sure we'll be able to fix something with them, because the island needs tourists and the tourists need a well run hotel. I'm sorry about Ben, but you'd better get him into the Welfare as soon as possible. I believe their terms are fairly reasonable for these days.'

'Old Ben's worth it to us,' said Grandpa. 'We've never been parted for a day since we got him as a puppy from the Battersea Dog's Home. He'd been found wandering on a motorway. It's downright wicked the way some people just dump animals like that. I'd dump *them* if I had the chance!'

Mr. Parker looked a bit startled as Grandpa thumped his fist on the desk and Billy, who was almost dizzy with relief and excitement, grinned right across his face. He'd heard it all dozens of times before, because one thing that always got Grandpa going was animals being badly treated.

'I'm sorry there's no where for you to live,' Mr. Parker sprang across the office, seized some papers the girl was silently holding out to him, read them in a flash and signed while he went on talking, 'but we haven't even got a spare chalet and . . .'

'Tent,' said Grandpa just as quickly as Mr. Parker.

'And it may be difficult to find . . . A tent! Yes, of course. Excellent idea. It's a nice little camping site right down by the sea. Go and see Mr. Tony in the bank in Albert Street. He rents out tents. He does ice creams as well in his spare time. Now if you could start tomorrow at 7.30 a.m., Mr. Luft,'

'Yes,' shot in Grandpa.

'. . . and if young Bobby wants to earn . . .'

'Billy,' put in Billy, who was starting to get the hang of talking to Mr. Parker.

' . . . that's right, Billy, if you want to earn some pocket money we're always short of people to wash up. It's paid by the hour. You can report to the kitchens about mid-day. All right? Now if you'll excuse me . . .'

He was already lifting up the phone with one hand while he went on signing papers with the other.

'This is the strangest place *I've* ever come across,' Grandpa said as the three of them set out for Albert Street. 'A policeman who gets you jobs through the lighthouse keeper! A chap in the bank selling ice creams! Where will it all end?'

'Don't forget the Animal Welfare Market,' put in Billy. 'I suppose they just sell the animals that haven't got homes. There's that cross girl again . . .'

He had seen her yesterday when she was with the lady who, rather like Mr. Parker, talked a lot. The girl was sitting on a bench looking grumpily at the tennis court. She had her arms folded and her fringe was right down over her eyes so that she was a little like Ben. Billy tried a half smile, but she only glared back so he made a face and ran to catch up with Grandpa who was striding along talking happily to himself.

'And I've seen a few odd places in my life I can tell you. Like the time I was sailing down the Orinoco River in South America and we saw this crocodile. As long as a London bus it was and *jaws*! Well, you wouldn't have believed it!'

It was a good story and although Billy had heard it before he listened with great attention because the moment was getting nearer and nearer when Ben would have to go into care.

The little nurse was waiting for them and she said briskly, 'Hallo. I've got everything ready for Ben. My sister rang to say you'd be up.'

'Sister?' said Grandpa. He'd gone a bit white under his tan again and he was holding on tightly to Ben's lead.

'She works for Mr. Parker at the Grand Harbour.

73

Come along, Ben. Now you're going to see a lot of me and we're going to be very good friends.'

She crouched down in front of Ben and went on talking to him in a low voice while she stroked him gently behind the ear. Ben went 'Hm hm hm' a few times and then leant heavily against her. He only did that to people that he liked so it was a good sign.

'You come along with me, then,' she said and somehow the lead was passed across to her without Grandpa really wanting to let go and he said in a gruff voice.

'Here's his shawl, he doesn't like being parted from it. And his bowl. What time can we come in and see him?'

'Anytime you like as long as its not too late at night. The vet's coming over soon and I'll ask him to give Ben a look over.'

Although she was being very kind and they were going to see Ben again in a matter of hours, it was a beastly moment when they saw him go plodding off with his large feet thumping on the cobbled courtyard. Even Winston had gone quiet for once and was just running sideways up and down his tree shaking his head.

'Oh, and Billy,' the nurse called over her shoulder, 'as I am rather overcrowded at the moment, it would be a great help if you could walk Boddie for me. Perhaps this evening after you've seen Ben . . .'

'Yup,' said Billy, 'O.K.'

'Clear off!' shrieked Winston.

Grandpa and Billy took his advice and walked off quickly in silence. It was as if part of them was missing, because Ben had always been with them wherever Grandpa had worked. They found the bank without any trouble and Grandpa almost stopped scowling when he saw a notice on the counter which read 'Fresh eggs for sale daily'. There were only a few customers and Mr. Tony, a pleasant faced young man, said that as it was coming up to his lunch hour he'd give them a lift down to the camping site so they could see which tent they'd like.

'Actually there's only two still vacant,' he said, 'so you're in luck. It looks as if it's going to be quite a good season, touch wood and spit on the sky. We need the tourists. The island largely lives through the winter on what it makes in the summer. Most of the hotels close down towards the end of September.'

He went on talking, but Billy was hardly listening. He was staring at Mr. Tony's car. It was quite unlike any vehicle he had ever seen before. It looked for all the world like an overgrown toy. It was about the size of a Mini, was bright scarlet and had a square bonnet and a square body with a canvas roof which unzipped at the back.

'It's a Skimp. Home-made,' said Mr. Tony proudly. 'I've had one or two slight problems, but it does all right for the island. Hop in the back, Billy, and hang on to the roof support otherwise you might fall out.'

There was only a narrow sort of metal shelf to sit on and Mr. Tony rolled up the whole of the back canvas and tied it up on the roof with tapes, so that there was nothing between Billy and the outside world but air.

Grandpa and Mr. Tony climbed into the front and off they went, and Billy saw at once why he had got to hang on tight because the little van-car fairly bounced along over the cobbles and Billy bounced with it. There was no time to feel sad about Ben being led away because he had to concentrate on not being bounced black and blue as they rattled and roared down the steep hill to the harbour and then flung round to the right and onto a smoother road which ran along beside the sea. Mr. Tony was an unusual sort of driver as he stuck firmly in the middle of the road, took corners at speed and waved constantly to people who were walking or cycling.

Clamping his teeth together to stop them juddering, Billy tried to lift some of the weight off his seat which was taking quite a lot of punishment on the metal shelf. He caught a glimpse of the cross girl trailing a bucket and spade as she walked towards the sands. She stared after them and Billy would have waved, but they went right over a large bump at that moment and he rose clean off the shelf and hit his head on the canvas roof and he was very glad that he was holding on with two hands.

'You still there?' Mr. Tony shouted, looking over his shoulder and not at the road ahead.

'Do you have a lot of accidents here?' Grandpa asked as Mr. Tony turned back again just in time to avoid a small girl on a very large, placid horse who had come plodding out of a side turning.

'Hardly any. Sometimes a telegraph pole seems to come out of the hedge and hit a car, but that's about all. This is Greengates.'

Greengates must have been one of the smallest villages in the world. There were three houses on either side of the road, a telephone kiosk, a bus shelter, a notice on a wall which read 'Eas and Offee' and a very old black labrador fast asleep in the middle of the road. It didn't even flip an ear as they drove round it.

'The campsite is just round the next bend,' said Mr. Tony, taking both hands off the wheel to point. Grandpa shut his eyes and bit hard on his pipe, but Billy was gazing in astonishment at two *more* castles which had just come into view, one of which looked quite a bit like the one he was determined to find. But then it too vanished out of sight as the Skimp turned down a fork in the road, narrowly missed a post office van which hurriedly drove into the bracken when it saw Mr. Tony coming, and turned off along a dirt

track past some cows which went on eating and finally came to a halt on the edge of a small field where there were a number of tents.

Billy and Grandpa got out rather stiffly and looked at them. They were large enough to have a living room and two bedrooms, a shower and a kitchenette. They had beds and cupboards and chairs and floor covering and windows and Grandpa, who hadn't been looking forward very much to 'camping out', perked up and began to look a little more cheerful.

Billy wandered off and climbed the high grassy bank at one side of the field to find the sea only a short

distance away. They were right on the edge of a small, curving bay with a castle at either end of it and a small island to one side. Billy let out a deep sigh of relief. It was going to be difficult to get used to not having Ben with him all the time, but he wasn't more than couple of miles away, and it was going to be fun living in a tent, exploring the island and swimming, and although he hated washing up, at least it would be a way of earning some money.

And tomorrow he would start looking for the vanishing castle . . .

7 · Boddie

The first visit to Ben wasn't too bad. He was very, very pleased to see them and nearly knocked Billy off his feet, but he whined a lot at the back of his throat when they had to leave. He was in a separate part of the Home where he had a small hut (with his shawl and bowl) to himself and a large piece of ground that was all fenced in.

'Ah, there you are,' said the little nurse as Billy stumped past the main building with his hands in his pockets. Grandpa had gone on ahead as one of the campers had told him about a man who hired out motor scooters and Grandpa had thought it might be a good idea to hurry round and see him.

'Yup.'

'Glad I've caught you. Here's Boddie waiting for you.'

Billy had completely forgotten that he was dog walking and he didn't want to do it much, but there was no way out and the nurse had been very kind about Ben.

'Don't let her off the lead until you're out of town.

She's not properly trained yet and some of the island drivers aren't very good.'

Billy thought of Mr. Tony and grinned. So did Boddie. She quite definitely smiled as she threw herself at him, got her legs tangled and fell over in a yelping heap. She was quite different from Ben who was rather sedate and slow at his advanced age. Boddie seemed to want to go in all directions at the same time. She got herself tied up in her lead, she raced round and round Billy so that *he* got tied up and then she nearly strangled herself round a lamp post. Half an hour with Boddie was about the same as a week with Ben and by the time they reached the cricket pitch in front of the Grand Harbour, Billy was

puffing and blowing. The moment she was off the lead Boddie jumped in the air and then went racing off, all legs and paws, and ran straight into a woman and a girl who were just appearing over the edge of the pitch.

'Boddie,' shouted Billy. 'Boddie, come back here!'

He might just as well have shouted at the wind for all the good it did. Boddie didn't even check for a second but leapt at the girl, barking at the top of her voice. The girl sat down with a thump, the woman tried to grab Boddie who went on down the steep hill towards the harbour. Billy panted past trying to pretend that it was all nothing to do with him and that he was just out for a run.

'Hi! I say! You!' the woman called, sounding a bit like Winston. But Billy kept on going. In fact by now he couldn't have stopped if he'd wanted to, as his feet were pounding along faster and faster as the hill got steeper and steeper. One foot caught in a piece of trailing bracken and Billy went over with a tremendous thump which knocked all the breath out of him. Luckily the ground was covered in springy turf and spongy ant heaps so he didn't hurt himself, but he couldn't move either until he had stopped seeing stars and got his breath back.

A rough tongue licked the side of his face and Billy opened his eyes to see Boddie looking down at him with her tail waving like a flag in a high wind.

'Umph,' grunted Billy and took a firm hold on her lead and struggled to his knees.

'That'll look like old Mrs. Rihoy's dog, Booodica,' said a voice and Billy saw a small, square shaped old man coming up through a path in the bracken. He had very round blue eyes and a net slung over his shoulder, and when Billy stood up he discovered that they were about the same height.

'Her name's Boddie,' Billy said.

'Ah, that'll be it. Real name, Booodica. Needs training she does then she'll be a good little dog. Teach her to rat, you could. There's always a need for good ratting dogs on the island.'

The old man bobbed his head and went on

climbing up the steep path as easily as if it were a flat road. Billy and Boddie followed on behind, taking care to leave the path and go round the edge of the cricket pitch in case the woman and the girl were still about.

'Well, you *have* taken her for a good walk,' said the nurse. Billy thought of saying that it was the other way round and Boddie had taken him for a good run, but the nurse was going on. 'Ben's settled down very happily for the night and he's snoring his head off. See you tomorrow, Billy.'

Billy started on what felt like the very long walk back to the camping site. After all it *had* been a very long day, but he hadn't gone more than a hundred yards or so when a very small car drew up alongside him and a cheerful voice said.

'Hallo. You'll be Billy Luft I expect. I'm the assistant lighthouse keeper. PC Martin and I had a word about your Grandpa.'

The man put out his hand and shook Billy's.

Billy hesitated. Ever since he could remember, Grandpa had told him never to take lifts from strangers and, after all, he couldn't be sure that this man *was* the lighthouse keeper, although he had a very nice, rather unusual face with dark, curly eyebrows.

'It's all right,' the keeper said, 'I'm not a kidnapper, but obviously you can't take *my* word for it. Oi!'

He leaned out of the window and shouted to a couple of fishermen who were hauling a boat up the beach, 'is it OK for me to give Billy a lift, seeing that he doesn't know me?'

'What! Not know Diddy?' one of the men roared back, 'everybody knows you. Is the weather going to hold Diddy?'

'Yes, for a while yet. There's a high coming in across the Atlantic.'

'You'll be OK, lad' the man shouted, 'I heard your Grandpa's got Fred Quevain's job up the Grand Harbour. Good luck to him.'

Billy felt a bit of an idiot as he climed into the tiny car, but he was also surprised all over again as to how fast news travelled on the island. Although he and Grandpa were strangers here it was as if they already belonged. It was a very nice feeling and he suddenly found himself talking to the keeper, Mr. Diddy, as if they were old friends.

'I'm sure I saw this great castle when we sailed in. It had two turrets and it was very large and it stuck right out into the sea.'

'Can't say I can place it,' said Mr. Diddy who, like Mr. Tony, drove in the middle of the road and kept waving at people. 'Mind you, one way and another, there *are* 14 forts and castles on and around the island, but there's only four that are set out on causeways and it doesn't sound like any of them.

Perhaps it was the sea mist. Mist can be a very mysterious thing.'

Suddenly Billy was too exhausted to do more than nod and by the time they reached the camping site he was three parts asleep. Mr. Diddy drove off with a friendly wave and Grandpa had already got the evening meal cooking.

They sat outside the tent to eat and one of the horses from up the lane who had pulled its tether loose came wandering past swishing its tail. A large seagull settled on top of the tent and a line of cows went past on their way to be milked. Billy said he'd help with the washing up, but Grandpa said he thought bed would be a better idea and Billy was asleep before his head was properly on his pillow, while Grandpa sat outside having a final cup of tea and watching the stars come out. He had always been a wanderer, but like Billy he felt as if he belonged on the island.

'Ah, but then there won't always be the work here,' he said with a sigh and made for bed himself.

Billy slept on and on in the morning and he didn't even hear Grandpa go to work on his rented red motor scooter. The sun was high in the sky by the time he woke up properly, and he decided that instead of having a shower he'd go for a swim. Billy had bathed only three days ago in the not too chilly and rather seaweedy water in the last place where

Grandpa had worked. The sea here looked quite different as it was very blue and quite clear with hardly a ripple on it. There were a few people sitting on the sand and some small children without any clothes on, paddling.

'Yipee,' thought Billy and he kicked off his shoes, dropped his towel and raced down the sand and into the sea. He was in and falling forwards and thrashing about before he could stop himself and it was a terrible shock. The water was freezing cold.

'Yow!' shouted Billy, and rose straight up like a jumping fish. He fell back and the second time under wasn't quite so bad and he decided to stay in, but to swim as fast as he could. Grandpa had taught him to swim when he was quite small and he wasn't bad at it, and after a minute or so he forgot the coldness and struck out for the tiny island. It was rocky round the edges and the water was glassy clear. Billy would have liked to explore it, but he was suddenly so hungry he felt as if he might pass out if he didn't have some food immediately.

Grandpa had left him a note reminding him about the washing-up job and some sausages and bacon and bread, and by the time all that was cooked, eaten and cleared away Billy thought he had better set out for the Grand Harbour. A nice, fat lady in a van gave him a lift and said she'd heard from her friend in the

Post Office that Billy's grandpa had got Fred Quevain's job and she hoped he'd like it.

'Of course the season's only just beginning,' she said, 'but we all hope it'll be a good one because we need the tourists. I *was* sorry to hear about your dog. But they're very good at the Animal Welfare. Here we are, then. I'm off to play tennis. Best of luck, Bobby.'

'Billy,' said Billy, but the lady had already picked up her racket from the back of the car and walked off to the tennis court where three friends were waiting for her.

'Hallo Mavis, hallo Maureen, hallo Joan. Sorry if I'm a bit late, but I've been talking to that boy who's dog's been put in quarantine. Yes, *isn't* it a shame!'

Billy felt as if everybody was looking at him as he edged his way into the entrance of the Grand Harbour. He scowled, looking just like Grandpa, and slid up to the Reception Desk where the girl with long fair hair was talking to Mr. Parker. He spotted Billy at once.

'Good to see you. Grandpa said you'd be along. I'll deal with those calls later. The kitchen's expecting you. Ask for Pete. Through that door.'

Billy was through the door and out the other side before he quite knew what was happening. It was very noisy and steamy in the kitchen with what seemed like dozens of people hurrying about in all directions and at first nobody took any notice of him and then quite a young person in a tall hat and a long white apron came up to him and said in a foreign sort of voice, 'You are Billy? Yes? If you will wash up over here? This is your apron and these are your gloves. The water is very hot, so look out. And please rinse carefully. It's just about two hours work and then we all have our meal. OK? I am Pete. Best wishes.'

Billy had been thinking that he would probably miss Ben quite a lot today and he had been a bit glum on the beach because Ben loved the sea, but since then there just hadn't been any time and there certainly wasn't now. Billy was surrounded by people washing up and talking at the tops of their voices and there was the most tremendous clatter of dishes and knives and forks and spoons all being emptied into the washing-up bowl. He didn't like to talk to any of the others as they were all quite a bit older than he was so when they shouted across to him he pretended to be extra busy. It got hotter and hotter although all the doors were open and he had to keep wiping his arm across his face. He hadn't asked Grandpa how much it was going to cost to keep Ben in the Welfare, but he knew it was bound to be quite a lot so the money had to be earned. And then suddenly everything slowed down and Pete called out.

'OK. Everything can go into the machines now. Everybody sit down. It's time for us to eat.'

Several of the other washer-uppers cheered and clapped and one of them beckoned to Billy to come and sit down at the end of a long table. He wondered how he could have ever felt cold in the sea because he was boiling hot now. And breakfast seemed a lifetime ago. The lunch was spaghetti bolognese and as much ice cream as he could eat – which was quite a lot – and when Billy reeled away from the table to help put their plates in the machine he didn't think he would ever be hungry again.

'Very good!' said Pete, 'I hope you'll come in again tomorrow? I'm sorry to hear about your dog. See you soon then, OK?'

Billy went and sat on a bench in front of the hotel to get his breath back. Everything was happening so fast. In only a very few hours he would be at the Animal Welfare to talk to Ben and then there would be Boddie to exercise and he hadn't seen Grandpa at all today. So what were they going to do about supper? Not that he was at all interested in food at the moment. But he did want to go and find the mysterious castle.

'Hallo,' said a gruff voice.

Billy looked up and saw the cross girl standing in front of him. If anything she looked even more cross now.

'What've you been doing?' she asked. 'You look hot enough to melt.'

'Washing up in the kitchens. It's hot as a stove in there.'

'Washing *up*?' The girl made it sound as though it was a really weird thing to do, and she stared at him harder than ever. 'Are you very poor?' she went on in a whisper. If it were possible Billy's face turned even redder. He glared at the girl and then ducked past her and began to walk round the side of the hotel to look for Grandpa. He felt in a furious temper all of a sudden and when the girl came running up to him for two pence he would have pushed her into the swimming pool.

'I'm sorry,' she said, not really sounding it, 'but you always seem to be doing something interesting and I'm so bored.' And she kicked at one of the white painted stones which lined the gravel path. It was very firmly embedded in the ground and the next second she was hopping round on one foot shouting, 'Ouch ouch ouch'. There's nothing like somebody else making a fool of themselves to make you feel better and Billy's own bad temper vanished.

'Hard luck,' he said, 'but there's such a lot to do. I mean swimming and exploring and going to see Ben and then there's Boddie and the tent and. . .' Billy stopped dead as he remembered the mysterious castle. He didn't think he was going to tell the girl about *that*. At least not yet.

'Who's Ben? Who's Boddie? What tent?'

She must have been the only person left on the island who hadn't heard about the rabies scare and Grandpa getting Mr. Quevain's job, let alone that they were living on the camping site. The girl was a good listener so Billy made it all sound a bit more dramatic than it really was, and when he told her about how he'd run away her mouth dropped open.

'Oh, you *are lucky*!' she said at the finish, 'nothing like that's ever happened to *me*! I just live in an ordinary house and my Dad's got an ordinary job and I'm on holiday with my Aunt Jackie.' Her face brightened up a bit. 'She's all right, but she don'ts.'

'*What*?'

'Don'ts. *You* know. *Don't* stay in the sea too long or you'll get cold. *Don't* read in bed for more than half an hour or you'll strain your eyes. *Don't* forget to put on suntan oil or you'll get burnt. I wouldn't mind washing up, but I bet she'd say don't about that too.'

'What's it like staying in the hotel?' Billy asked quickly. She'd begun to look gloomy again. He had never stayed in one himself, and he couldn't imagine it.

'It's all right. I've got a telly in my bedroom and my own bathroom. But everybody else seems quite old and all they do is play tennis and eat and talk. *You* know.'

Billy wasn't sure that he did as it was all quite a different life from anything he had ever known. He wouldn't have minded living in an ordinary house for a bit, just to see what it was like waking up every morning in the same bedroom. And going to a regular school and having friends must be OK.

'I'll tell you something if you promise not to laugh,' the girl said suddenly. Billy was only half listening as he'd just spotted Grandpa at the top of a ladder working on some guttering.

'Mm.'

'My name,' said the girl, scowling so that her fringe came right down to her eyes and she looked like Ben, 'My name's *Petal*.' She said it with loathing. It really didn't suit her as she was a very solid sort of girl.

'And mine's Billy,' said Billy, wondering what all the fuss was about, 'Come and meet Grandpa. And after that I'll tell *you* something.'

Billy was determined to prove that he had seen the castle and he had suddenly made up his mind that he needed help and Petal was it!

8 · Petal

'It's like a *real* adventure,' Petal said.

Because she was lonely and bored she had asked Billy dozens of questions and she could hardly believe that she now knew somebody who had once lived with a circus and who had wandered all over the country going from town to town wherever the work was. Petal wasn't too sure what her Aunt Jackie would make of it all so she just told her that she was going to the shops to look for something to read. Billy, who was standing quite close, heard the aunt say, '*don't* forget to look both ways before you cross the road. And *don't* talk to strangers.'

'There's not much traffic here,' he said, 'and everybody seems to know everybody else or be their relation or something so I don't see how they *can* be strangers. What are you going to get to read?'

'A map,' said Petal, 'I didn't actually say a book, I just said something to read, so it wasn't a lie. I've seen the maps up in Walters' Shop. It's bound to show all the castles and then we can find your one.'

Billy was a bit put out that the idea hadn't

occurred to him, but it was clever of Petal to think of it and he was generous enough to say so.

'That's OK,' said Petal, skipping up the cobbled street, 'If you hadn't told me you were a visitor like me I'd have thought you'd always lived here. You look like everybody else.'

A gaggle of boys were cycling down the street with their fishing rods strapped across their backs. They were tanned and fair-haired and tough looking and wiry rather than tall and Billy remembered the fit old man who had walked up the path carrying a net. He'd been bit like Grandpa.

'I expect it's being out of doors a lot,' Billy said. 'Is this the shop? I hope a map doesn't cost a lot.'

Mr. Walters, who owned the shop which seemed to sell everything from soap to birthday cards, was dodging about in the same energetic way as Mr. Parker did.

'A map?' he said. 'A map. A map. A map. Yes, I think we have several if not more of those. Let me just see.'

He dived behind one of the counters, served several people with magazines and cards and talked all the time as he rummaged through a large box.

'And your boxing magazine, sir. Five cards? Certainly madam. And your knitting book, my dear. A map. A map. A map. Yes, dozens of maps. Take your choice and you can pay me later. No, the

Journal doesn't come out until tomorrow I'm afraid, my dear. Shall we keep you one? Go like hot cakes the Journals do. Found the map you want yet? Yes, a very good choice. . .'

Billy and Petal practically reeled out of the shop and then went and spread the map on the low wall in front of a café where people were having coffee on the terrace. A dog, a little like Ben, but much younger, went thumping past and Billy sighed without meaning to. When you've always had a dog with you it leaves a big gap when he's not there any longer.

'What a lot of castles,' Petal was saying. 'I always thought it was a small island, but it's quite big if you've got to walk it all.'

They both felt a bit daunted, because for half-an-hour after the map idea the mysterious castle had seemed to be almost within their reach, but now it was slipping away again. A party of yachtsmen settled themselves at a table nearby and they heard one of them say, 'the water round here really is tricky. All those currents and then there's the sea mist. That's very deceptive.'

'Yes, if you can't see the beacons, you have to let the Harbour master's office talk you in.'

Billy, most of his attention on the map, wondered if the beacons were like the big bonfires that were lit on Guy Fawkes' night.

'Well, the weather seems set fair for a while.

There's a high coming in from the west,' another voice said.

And what *was* a high? If he saw that lighthouse keeper again he'd ask him. Or perhaps Grandpa would know.

'I think I'm having another idea,' said Petal, who had started frowning again and getting her Ben look. 'Bicycles. We could hire some.'

'Aunt Don't won't let you,' Billy said before he could stop himself. 'And anyway I bet they cost a bomb.' It was strange how often things came back to money.

'Aunt *what?* Oh, *don't!*' Petal giggled. 'She needn't know. Let's go and ask anyway.'

The cycle hiring shop was down a small side street and the man who ran it shook his head and said that he was a bit short on cycles at the moment.

'There's a lot of people coming in you see. The harbour's getting bang tight with yachts and the moment they come ashore they're all for hiring a bike. And I get rushed off my feet. Not that I'm complaining, but they're practically all out apart from some that need repairs and that.'

'Perhaps I could have a look at 'em,' said Billy.

Grandpa had been teaching him how to mend things and how to look after things ever since he could remember. Grandpa was so good at it himself that he always made it seem easy whether it was carpentry or plumbing, electricity or painting and a lot of it had been absorbed by Billy. When the cycle man took them into a side barn and showed him the casualties, he thought he could cope with them.

'Well then,' the man said, 'if you make a job of 'em you can have two free of charge per day. Hold on, haven't you been walking old Mrs. Rihoy's dog, Boddie? Needs training that dog does. The little nurse, she hasn't got time to walk it regular.'

The man absent-mindedly passed a repair kit over to Billy and settled himself more comfortably on a barrel. He didn't look as if he was all *that* rushed off his feet. Petal spread out the map and crouched down cross-legged to read it as Billy started tinkering.

'Hold it again,' the man went on, although nobody else was talking. 'That's the ticket. It'll be your grandpa that's got Fred Quevain's job at the Grand Harbour while Fred's daughter's over from Australia.'

Billy nodded and eased the brake blocks on a Red Racer. The next thing would be that the man would tell him that he was living on the camping site and that Ben was in kennels. It was very strange how people told you things about yourself when quite obviously you knew much more about you than *they* did! But the man veered off onto another tack.

'And you'll be staying with your Aunty at the Grand Harbour,' he informed Petal who looked very surprised. 'Ah, you'll be wondering how I know. My niece she done your aunty's hair at the hairdressers' last week and your Aunty said you were finding it quiet.'

'Not now,' said Petal.

Billy dropped a hammer with a crash. He didn't want their plan to find the vanishing castle to be spoken about all round the island. People might think he was dotty or childish.

'We're going exploring,' said Petal, smiling wickedly and looking quite different from the cross girl of earlier in the day, '*and* we're going to try and train Boddie.'

That was a new one on Billy, but he accepted it without a blink and returned to his repair work. It took longer than he'd bargained for, but the cycle man, who was now sitting behind his shop counter reading a newspaper, was so delighted that he said.

'Bang up job you've made of those Red Racers. Hold it a moment. I tell you what. How'd you feel about coming in say twice a week for a couple of hours just to do a maintenance job? I'd pay, of course, and you and your friend can ride free. Is it a deal?'

Billy thought it over. That would mean *two* jobs which would all help to keep Ben in the kennels. It made him feel rich and responsible.

'OK,' Billy said and they shook hands on it.

'Pity you and your Grandpa don't live here regularly,' the man said, settling back after they'd fixed up the money side of things. 'We could do with more handymen on the island. But you can't get the workers these days. They're all off to the mainland to earn the big money. Some of the forts are in crying need of repair work. Take Fort Poidevin for a start . . .'

But where they were to take it Billy and Petal never found out because some yachtspeople came into the shop at that moment and the cycle man had to do some work.

The little nurse was delighted to see them and Ben came hurrying up to the wire on his large feet and licked and licked Billy's hand and Billy gave him a hug and buried his face in Ben's thick grey fur for a moment.

'Hm hm hm hm hm,' Ben said at the back of his throat and he lumbered off and got his shawl to show it to Petal, which was a great honour. Boddie nearly went out of her head with pleasure and fell over twice before they finally managed to make her understand that she was to trot along *beside* the bicycle and not in *front* of it.

'She really is *silly*,' Petal said crossly. It was Petal's cycle that Boddie had upset twice and Petal had scraped her knee.

'No she's *not*! She's just untrained!' Billy flared up.

For a moment it looked as if a quarrel was brewing and then Boddie saw a rabbit and went after it like a greyhound. She didn't catch it, for which Billy was grateful as he wouldn't have known what to do with it if she had. So time was getting on when they reached the first castle which Petal had marked on the map. It was a bit disappointing as it was very square in shape, had no turrets, a bolted front door, a dry moat full of blackberry bushes and was most definitely well and truly on solid ground, and set well back from the sea. So they crossed it off the list, which left only thirteen to go.

Of course it soon became quite impossible to keep what was going on from Grandpa, let alone Aunty Don't. So Billy and Petal decided to tell them half the story, which was that they were exploring and training Boddie at the same time. Grandpa took all this without a blink. He had been rather quiet the last few days as though his mind were on other things.

'Just don't do anything foolish like trying to climb down the cliffs,' he said. 'Boddie's a nice little dog. Not a touch on Ben though. You like it here, don't you, Billy?'

'Yes, lots. It's . . .' Billy waved his arms.

'Yes, I feel like that too.'

Grandpa put his pipe in his mouth and pushed his spectacles onto the top of his head.

'The trouble is, there doesn't seem to be much

regular work. And Mr. Quevain'll be back to work at the Grand Harbour in the Autumn and most of the other hotels'll close down for the winter and we can't live on what you earn at the bicycle shop and washing up, although it's a great help. Still, perhaps something'll come along. Now as Winston would say, hop it.'

Billy hopped. Aunty Don't was quite a different kettle of fish. She thought of about six different reasons why Petal shouldn't go exploring or cycling or trying to train an unknown dog. Fortunately Mr. Parker overheard all this as he was racing through the Residents' Lounge. He stopped so suddenly that Billy half expected to hear the sound of screeching brakes.

'Morning,' he said brightly. 'I hear you're doing well in the kitchen, Billy, *and* at the cycle shop. You take after your Grandpa all right. He's a marvellous worker. And now you're going to start dog training. Well done.' He turned to Petal's aunt who was looking dissapproving. 'Don't you agree that it's a very good thing for young people to take on jobs like that? It teaches them the value of money for a start and keeps them from doing silly things. You must be very proud of Petal.'

'I . . .' said Aunty Don't.

'Exactly,' agreed Mr. Parker as though she actually *had* agreed with him, 'well, we mustn't keep them. You know the bridge tournament starts today?'

'I don't . . .' Aunty Don't managed before Mr. Parker rolled on.

'Don't expect you've had time to put your name down for it so I did it for you. The first prize is a special dinner for four. Perhaps *you'll* win it! Well, must dash.'

And he did, straight through the lounge and past Billy and Petal and Boddie who were getting out while they had the chance. Mr. Parker gave them a wink and a wave, jumped lightly into his open jeep and went roaring off down the drive.

The second castle was a little more promising than the first in that it did have a causeway and was built about five hundred yards out to sea. But it had no turrets and no frontdoor and when Billy cautiously edged inside he discovered at once that it had no floor either.

'Cripes,' he said, flinging his arm round the brickwork and looking down through the shadowy darkness to a very black sea about twenty feet below. It was lapping backwards and forwards so that the fort was full of the sound of slapping water and Billy took a deep breath as he realised how close he'd come to dropping into what would undoubtedly be a very dangerous trap. He looked quite pale as he edged his way back into the hot sunlight, but Petal didn't notice as she and Boddie had clambered out over the rocks to where a small old man was fishing. Six extremely large, black-feathered birds were hunched on a big rock out to sea watching him.

'Noon,' the old man said and then as Billy came slithering over, 'Oh, it's you again. We met on the goat track below the cricket pitch, but I didn't know who you were then although you looked familiar. Quevain, Fred Quevain.'

It seemed strange to meet him properly after they had heard so much about him. He showed them the bass he'd caught and pointed out the swirls and ripples round the rocks, the good places for fish.

'Everybody on the island who fishes has their own special spot,' he said, 'and they likes to keep it secret so don't you go telling anyone that this is mine!' And he put his finger alongside his nose and winked one round, blue eye. Billy asked him what a high meant and was told that it was an area of high pressure coming in across the Atlantic which would break up all the clouds. And as for beacons, they were like miniature lighthouses, but set back so that a boat's captain coming in could line up on two of them and work out exactly where he was on his chart.

Billy glanced at Petal who had taken off her sandals and was sitting on a narrow ledge dangling her feet in the very deep water in a way which would have made Aunty Don't have a fit. Billy decided to

take the plunge and after a couple of false starts he described the mysterious castle that he had seen from the boat.

'Ah,' said Mr. Quevain, not looking in the least surprised or as if he thought Billy was daft, 'that's not the first time I've heard that tale.'

Billy nearly fell off the rock.

'Islands are always full of stories about shipwrecks and pirates, treasurers and rescues. All my life I've been hearing 'em. My old Granny Cosheril was always telling them. Now how did that particular one go? Hold on, I've got a bite.' And sure enough another silvery brown bass came leaping out of the choppy blue waves.

'Ah,' said Mr. Quevain when the fish had been dealt with and had joined the others in their neat row. 'It *was* something to do with the sea mist being thick and if a boat was in trouble and 'got two turrets in a line then a castle and a mine' then they'd be safe round the Swinge Rocks. Of course it's all talk. Sailors' talk. I never saw it myself, mind, this fortress castle of yours, but it must have been there once or people wouldn't have remembered it.'

'What sort of mine?' Petal asked. 'Gold? Silver? Diamonds?'

'That I couldn't say. I never heard of none of *them* on the island. Well, I must be off. You keep my secret and I'll keep yours.'

'Well, at least we know other people have seen it,' said Petal, watching the five black cormorants leave their rock and beat their way over the waves just a wing tip away from the water, 'that makes it a lot more real. Tomorrow we could try Fort Quinain and Mantell Castle. Quinain's at the end of a *very* long causeway, so perhaps that'll be it!'

But it wasn't. They had to wait for the low tide to get across the very long causeway to what from a distance looked so like what Billy remembered that he felt sure this was it! It had turrets, it was far out to sea and it seemed about the right shape. But when they did wheel their bicycles over – the causeway was covered by the sea twice in every twenty-four hours so it was extremely slippery – Billy could see at once that it wasn't right. It was just a very solid brick building and not in the least like the castle he had glimpsed. And as for Fort Mantell, that was just an enormous castle with no end of turrets, about ten altogether but it was set high up on the cliffs well above sea level.

One by one Petal crossed off the forts on the map as being no good. Billy washed up what seemed like hundreds of plates and cups and glasses, knives, forks and spoons and as more and more boats came into the harbour the island became fuller and fuller. So Billy showed Petal how to do some of the repairs on the bicycles. Grandpa and Mr. Parker both began to work harder and harder and Aunty Don't found herself busily helping to do teas down at the Sailing Club, playing in the Bridge Tournament and then before she knew quite how it happened, serving behind a stall at the Animal Welfare market.

'It's a strange thing,' said Aunty Don't, meeting Grandpa in the Reception Hall of the Grand Harbour, 'but I thought this was a very quiet little island when I first came here. But I've never been so busy before in my life. Are you all right Mr. Luft? You look quite pale under your tan. I do hope you haven't been overdoing it? Sit down for a moment. There's nothing the matter with Ben is there?'

Grandpa shook his head and took the cup of coffee Aunty Don't was holding out. The spoon rattled in the saucer.

'I was just taking a short cut through the churchyard,' Grandpa said, getting out his pipe and nearly biting through the stem, 'and I happened to glance at one of the old, *old* gravestones *and* . . .'

9 · The Mysterious Island

Billy and Petal were down to the last two castles and the last week of Petal's and Aunty Don't's holiday when Mr. Quevain offered to take them out in his boat, 'The Lilley Lihou'.

'Named after my Granny,' he said. 'There'll be a good fast tide running, and with all this warm weather there'll be shoals of fish about, you'll see. I'll be bringing up my lobster pots as well. And maybe we'll catch a sight of that mysterious castle of yours from the sea, same as you did last time.'

'Oh well,' said Aunty Don't, 'I'm sure Mr. Quevain knows what he's doing and you don't seem to have come to any harm so far. But *don't* lean over the side of the boat too far, that's all!'

'Are you doing OK in the bridge competition?' Billy asked politely.

'Well, yes, not too bad at all. Four, five, six, seven marrows and three dozen courgettes. Give me a hand with the table, Billy . . .'

Aunty Don't was putting out the vegetables with the islanders had given for the Animal Welfare market. It wasn't animals that were sold there at all, but fruit and veg. which people came and bought, and the money helped to keep the Welfare running. Aunty Don't arranged everything so beautifully that her stall was always the one that sold out first.

Billy went to have a few words with Ben who was lying in the shade snoring softly, but he woke up the moment that Billy opened his gate and rolled over and came padding across to lean against him.

'Hm hm hm hm,' he said.

Billy sat down on the warm grass and put his arms round him. Time which had once seemed to go past slowly had suddenly started to go faster and faster. Mr. Quevain's daughter was beginning to make plans to return to Australia and as soon as that happened Grandpa would lose his job. And in the Autumn the camping site would shut down and all the tents would vanish and they would have nowhere to live and no work, so they would have to go back to the mainland leaving Ben with the little nurse to finish the quarantine. That was all bad enough, but Boddie was just starting to learn how to behave properly and how would *she* manage without Billy taking her out every day?

'Oh well,' said Billy, 'something'll come along.'

He tried to sound cheerful, but he absolutely hated the thought of leaving the island and he knew Grandpa did too although they hadn't talked about it again. But then Grandpa had been behaving very strangely recently, going round muttering to himself and not seeming to hear when people spoke to him.

But Billy couldn't stay sad for long for long because it was the most wonderful day with the sea so blue it almost hurt to look at it and a roll of mist lying out on the horizon. He cycled down to the harbour, passing Constable Martin driving up in his van and then the lighthouse keeper in his little yellow and red car. Billy seemed to know every second person he saw and then he had to turn onto the pavement as Mr. Tony roared towards him in his red car right in the middle of the road.

Petal and Mr. Quevain were there ahead of him, walking down the slipway to the old inner harbour where the islanders anchored their fishing boats. The crane was squealing away further along the harbour wall, picking up the great boulders which came from the island quarries, to drop them over on the sea side of the wall as protection against the racing, roaring seas of the autumn and winter.

'Well, last two castles,' Petal said, spreading out the map which had become very tattered and worn. 'Fort Huret and Fort Poidevin.'

'There's talk,' said Mr. Quevain, hauling up the anchor, 'that some big mainland company has bought up Poidevin to turn it into flats. That'll be a job and a half. Nobody's done any work down there for years and years. Off we go, then.'

They chugged away under the lee of the wall, where the crane driver waved to them from his cab and then out to the open sea. Billy helped to haul in the lobster pots with their snapping cargo, but Petal didn't much care for the look of their claws and went and sat in the bow where Mr. Quevain's flag snapped and flapped. The gulls from the harbour followed them out, wheeling and dipping and hoping for pieces of fish.

'The Mark Land Trust I do believe the firm's called,' said Mr. Quevain, bringing the 'Lilley' round smartly as they started to chug through one of the fast currents that frothed between the rocks. 'PC Martin was telling me about it last night and he got it from the lighthouse and they always know *everything* up there. It'd be good if they could save the old fort and bring her back to life. My word, here comes a whopper.'

It was hard work bringing in the nets with their squirming, jumping load of fish, and everybody felt in need of a rest and a bite of something to eat by mid-day.

'There we are, "Fort Huret",' said the old man pointing.

It was the biggest castle they had seen so far, absolutely enormous and when he told them it had once housed two thousand soldiers seventy years ago, they could believe it. It was impressive all right, but it was set high up on the headland at least quarter of a mile from the sea, so it wasn't the right castle.

Billy shook his head and watched a little scarf of sea mist drift just over the surface. Then another and another.

'Mist's coming in fast,' said Mr. Quevain, 'we'd best head for the harbour.'

'Oh not yet, *please*,' said Petal, 'it's not far to Fort Poidevin is it? And it is the *last* castle . . .'

The old man hesitated and then shrugged his shoulders, set the engine going, and off they went straight into the mist. It was an eerie feeling because the mist cut off a lot of the sound and even the cries of the gulls faded away as they swooped higher and higher into the blue sky and soon there was nothing but the chug-chug of the engine and the slap of the waves. To Billy, it was as if time had slipped backwards and he was just catching sight of the whole mysterious island for the first time. There were just little patches of it to be glimpsed and the 'Lilley' began to roll as they sailed into the middle of the choppy current which was speeding between the rocks at the turn of the tide.

Billy leant over the side straining his eyes. He didn't know *why* it was so important to catch a glimpse of 'his' mysterious castle again, he just knew it *was*. It had become the most important thing in his life. And then, just as it had done before, a gap

appeared in the sea mist and as it was blown apart like billowing curtains, through the gap he could see the shimmering blue sea and beyond that the green and brown and yellow of the island. The mist slid across, thickened, billowed and whirled and the boat began to curve round, keeling over slightly. Billy darted across to lean on the other rail and as he did, so the mist just rolled up on itself. And there it was, the mysterious vanishing castle exactly as he had seen it before with its two gleaming turrets and its extraordinary shape as though it was a quarter of a mile long at least and coming straight towards them!

Billy got his breath back and yelled. Mr. Quevain cut the 'Lilley's' motor, Petal jumped about a foot off the coiled rope she'd been sitting on and they all three peered at the castle.

'You see, you see, you see,' was all Billy could manage. 'It *is* real. It *is* true, you see!'

'So I do,' said Mr. Quevain.

'Cripes!' said Petal.

'That's old Poidevin,' said Mr. Quevain, 'only in all my years I never seen her dead on like that. Well you *wouldn't*, going through this current! You'd be all eyes on straight ahead. But it's bang to rights like the old sailors used to say, 'you get two turrets in a line, then a castle, then a mine'. What you've got there is the beacon on the end of the Poidevin rocks, then the fort herself, then the beacon at the land end of the causeway and behind that the old stone quarry. Put it altogether and you've got what looks like a very odd castle indeed. Well, you've discovered in a few weeks what I've never seen before in 70 years! And what's more, if we don't look lively we'll be on the rocks ourselves in a minute of two. Hard about . . .'

The mist unfurled itself and blotted out the fort, and Billy sank back on his heels and closed his eyes. Neither Petal nor the old man liked to say anything as they chugged back very slowly towards the harbour. Billy looked as if he was asleep, but he wasn't, far from it. Everything he had heard and learnt since he came to the mysterious island was all falling into a kind of shape. He and Grandpa were going to live here with Ben and Boddie and all their other new friends and the solution to their problems was quite simple. All it needed was for him to do a bit of talking.

Grandpa was down at the harbour seeing to some unloading for Mr. Parker who, as usual, was bouncing about at twice the speed of everybody else. Grandpa heard Billy's shout as they chugged through and waved back, and if Billy hadn't been so full of his own affairs he would have noticed that Grandpa had become his old smiling, cheerful, talkative self.

'I've got something to tell you, Billy,' he said, giving Petal a helping hand to come ashore up the iron grid set in the wall.

'Grandpa, I know where you could get a job that . . .'

'Mr. Parker heard from the lighthouse, they know everything up there . . .'

'Would go on and on for years and there'd be somewhere for us to live and . . .'

'About these Mark Land Trust people taking over Fort Poidesomething.'

'Vin,' said Mr. Quevain, winking at Petal who was staring from Grandpa to Billy and back again. Nobody took any notice of him.

'And . . .' said Billy.

'And . . .' said Grandpa.

'Hallo,' said Mr. Parker, bouncing up and talking twice as fast and as loud as anybody else. 'Well that's all very satisfactory. The Mark Land Trust are going to take on Grandpa to work at Fort Poidevin, Billy. They're so impressed by all the work that he's done at the Grand Harbour, that they're putting him in charge of turning it into flats and getting it properly up to date and when *that's* all done you can stay on there in your own flat with Grandpa as Caretaker. What do you think of *that*?'

Billy just stared with his mouth open until Grandpa hit him on the back and then it was his turn to stare. He looked and looked at the 'Lilley Lihou' until his eyes were as round as Mr. Quevain's.

'That's the name I saw in the churchyard,'

Grandpa said hoarsely. 'It all came back to me. That was my mother's name before she got married and became Mrs. Luft.'

'Oh there's a lot of Lihous in these parts,' said Mr. Quevain who had been stolidly unloading his pots while all this was going on. 'My Gran was a Lilley Lihou as well, so you and me are probably related somewhere along the line. I always thought Billy looked like an island boy. He's standing around like one *too*, instead of giving me a helping hand . . .'

What seemed like a long, long time later, Billy and Petal went up to see Ben and to collect Boddie who promptly went head over heels.

'Well, well, well,' said the little nurse. 'I hear Grandpa's going to work for the Mark Land Trust people. Isn't that good news? I'm sure Boddie will love living in a fort.'

'*What?*'

'It's just what she needs, a nice, settled home,' the little nurse said briskly, 'with you and Grandpa to look after her.'

'Yes, well, oh!' said Billy. It was all happening too fast for him. He went and sat down with Ben who leant his shaggy muzzle on Billy's shoulder and went 'Hm hm hm'.

And it was *almost* as if he was saying,

'There, I *told* you something would come along – and it *has*!'

THE HAPPY GHOST

'Sam slipped upstairs to keep watch . . . .
Something moved in the blue-black shadows
of the garden . . . . The short hairs on the
back of Sam's neck went as stiff as the bristles
on a scrubbing brush. And then the shape
vanished . . . .'

From the attic window, Sam had a clear view
of the derelict cottages. Nobody lived there,
so why were there strange shapes and the
flickering lights inside. Had Sam seen some
horrific ghost which had come back to haunt
the scene of its dastardly crime?

THE TOVERS

Once upon a time the world was full of Tovers
– the Left-Over Little People of the world.
They were all quite different but they had
one thing in common – they lived in Rings.
But as the modern age approached and towns
and roads swallowed up the countryside, the
Rings were gradually swept away. Now there
was only one ancient Sanctuary Ring left.
How could the Tovers survive?

THE ANIMALS NOBODY WANTED

Paul and Rosa were not looking forward to their holiday on a lonely farm by the sea without their parents – though there was that old stone fort to explore. But when they follow the enormous ginger cat up the steep steps to Ballig Fort neither of them is prepared for the exciting secret world they uncover. Before long the children are involved in a battle to save and care for a whole zoo of wild creatures, including sea-birds damaged by oil, a jackdaw called Bertie and a friendly black labrador!